Terminal Shock

Letters began appearing on the video display one at a time, as though being pecked out slowly by a two-finger typist. The first word to appear was:

HELP!!

Frank sat bolt upright in his chair. "Something's wrong," he said.

"Is this a joke?" asked Joe.

"I don't think so," said Frank. "We have to see what else he types."

The brothers hovered in front of the computer. All they could do was watch as Jim finished typing his message. Finally it was complete. It read:

HELP!! I THINK I'M DYING!! COME TO MY HOUSE IMMEDIAAZZCV

Then the typing stopped. Jim Lerner's computer—or Jim Lerner himself—had gone completely dead!

The Hardy Boys Mystery Stories

Available from MINSTREL Books

TERMINAL SHOCK

FRANKLIN W. DIXON

PUBLISHED BY POCKET BOOKS

New York   London   Toronto   Sydney   Tokyo   Singapore

A MINSTREL PAPERBACK *ORIGINAL*

A Minstrel Book published by
POCKET BOOKS, a division of Simon & Schuster Inc.
1230 Avenue of the Americas, New York, NY 10020

ISBN: 0-671-69288-7

First Minstrel Books printing June 1990

10 9 8 7 6 5 4 3 2 1

THE HARDY BOYS MYSTERY STORIES is a trademark
of Simon & Schuster Inc.

THE HARDY BOYS, A MINSTREL BOOK and colophon are
registered trademarks of Simon & Schuster Inc.

Printed in the U.S.A.

Contents

Becky north:
    Demi Lavato

TERMINAL
SHOCK

Joe Hardy:
Kellan Lutz

Phil Cohen:
Ricky Ulman

Frank Hardy:
Shia Laboufe

Jim Lerner:
Daniel Radcliffe

1 On-line with Death

"You're crazy!" said Joe Hardy. "Absolutely bonkers!"

Blond, muscular Joe scowled at his friend Phil Cohen and waved a hand at him, as if to dismiss whatever it was that Phil had just told him. The two teenagers were standing on the sidewalk in front of Joe's house, under a cloudless blue sky. A cool breeze ruffled their hair.

"Aw, come on, Joe," said Phil, who was shorter and less muscular, with brown hair. "It was just a suggestion. And it might do you some good."

"Ha!" laughed Joe, though he wasn't smiling. "Me? Learn to program computers? That's the stupidest idea I've heard since—since—"

"It's not that stupid," protested Phil, who was

1

well known around Bayport High as an expert on all things electronic. "You're a smart guy. All that jock stuff—the football and everything—is good for your body, but you don't do enough for your brain. Besides, you need a hobby."

"I've got a hobby," said Joe. "Crime fighting. I'm a part-time detective, remember? And my brain gets all the exercise it needs in school."

"There you go!" said Phil triumphantly. "You're a detective. Computers could help you solve crimes."

"How?" asked Joe. "Maybe if I dropped one on a burglar's head . . ."

"You're not keeping up with the times," Phil said. "A lot of crimes are committed on computers now. Hackers breaking into computer systems and stealing credit card numbers. Spies learning state secrets. Students changing their grades on the school computer."

"Now, *that* sounds useful," said Joe. "Maybe you could show me how to do that."

Phil shook his head. "Joe, if you don't take this seriously, you're going to be useless as a crime fighter. You won't even understand how the crimes are committed, much less how to track down the criminals. Besides, you don't really have to learn to *program* a computer, just a thing or two about how they work. Come on over to my place and I'll show you the ropes."

"Nah," said Joe with a frown. "That's just not for me. Spring vacation just started, remember? I think

2

it's illegal to learn anything over vacation. Now, if you've got some good video games, that's different. I saw this great one the other day where you play a shark and you get points for eating swimmers. A hundred bonus points for a lifeguard."

"Oh, forget it," said Phil. "You're hopeless, Joe. Don't blame me if your detective career goes down the tubes."

"Hey!" said Joe. "I've been great without a computer until now, and I'll continue to be great."

"I'm not so sure of that," said Phil. "Anyway, I'll see you later. Say hi to your brother, Frank, for me."

"Will do," said Joe. "Take it easy."

Joe turned and started toward his front door. He looked up at the blue sky and wondered why Phil Cohen would think that he'd want to spend a day like this in front of a computer screen. It was a perfect day for baseball or football or running or just about anything else you could do outdoors.

He opened the front door. Even before he stepped inside he could smell the fragrant aroma of his aunt Gertrude's cooking. Roast beef and baked potatoes. The smell alone was enough to start his mouth watering. Ever since Joe's parents had left on a vacation trip to the West Coast three days earlier, Aunt Gertrude had been pampering Joe and his older brother, Frank, with some of the best meals she had ever cooked.

"Hey, Frank," Joe yelled, calling for his brother as he entered the foyer. "Let's grab a bat and ball

3

and head over to the field, play a few innings before dinner. You'll never guess what Phil Cohen said to me this afternoon!"

"I'm busy," replied his brother from somewhere upstairs. "Tell me later."

"Huh?" said Joe. "Don't tell me you're *studying* on a holiday. You'll ruin your eyes—and your social life."

He bounded up the stairs and peered through the door of his brother's room. Frank's bedroom was large and comfortable, with a sturdy wooden bed in the middle, surrounded by a large bureau and a desk and posters of athletes and movie stars. At the moment, however, the room was plunged into near darkness. Frank was sitting at the desk, hunched in front of a microcomputer. The bright green characters on the screen gave the darkened room an eerie glow and made Frank's face look ghoulish.

"Oh, no!" moaned Joe. "Not you, too! Everybody's turning into a computer nerd. Who am I going to play ball with?"

"Stick a sock in it," said Frank, glancing up from the computer screen. "I'm logging on to Jim Lerner's BBS. I'll be with you in a minute."

"You're *what?*" Joe asked. "That sounds like something Phil Cohen would do. Are you sure you're my brother?"

Frank looked up disgustedly, his dark eyes glowering underneath his thick brown hair. "I'm logging on to a BBS—a computerized bulletin board

4

system. Watch over my shoulder. Maybe you'll learn something."

"I don't want to learn anything," said Joe. "I'm on vacation. I just finished telling Phil that."

Suddenly a harsh roaring sound erupted from a small, flat device tucked under Frank's telephone, which was located next to the computer.

"What was that?" asked Joe, startled.

"That was my modem connecting with Jim's modem," said Frank.

"Your modem?" asked Joe. "I thought you were connecting with Jim's computer, not that funny electronic thing under the phone."

"The modem," explained Frank, "is what lets my computer connect with Jim's computer through the telephone. Now our computers can talk to each other. Clear?"

"Clear as an oil spill," said Joe. "What do your computers talk about?"

"Pay attention and you'll see," said Frank.

More bright green characters began to appear on the display, one at a time, as though someone were typing very rapidly on the keyboard. Frank's hands were not on the keyboard, however. Joe leaned over his shoulder and read:

WELCOME!
You have reached the
COSMIC CITADEL BBS
1200/2400/4800/9600 Baud

"Wow!" said Joe. "Is Jim Lerner typing that stuff?"

"His *computer* is typing that stuff," Frank said. "Then it sends it to my computer through the phone, and my computer displays it on the screen, where we can read it."

"What's a—a 'sysop'?" asked Joe, reading the word off the screen and pronouncing it "size op."

"That's pronounced 'sizz op,'" corrected Frank. "It's short for 'system operator.' It means the guy— or the girl—who runs the bulletin board system. Jim runs this board out of his house, so naturally he's the sysop. His girlfriend, Becky, is co-sysop, which means she helps him out with the board."

Just below the welcome message on the screen, the words *Your name?* had appeared. Following the question mark was a blinking square of light, which seemed to indicate that the computer was waiting for Frank to type something.

"So, are you going to tell it your name?" asked Joe.

"Uh-huh," said Frank. He typed *Frank Hardy* on the keyboard. Then he pressed a large key marked Enter. The words *Your password?* appeared on the next line. Frank typed something in response, but only dots appeared on the screen.

"Why'd you type those dots?" asked Joe.

"I didn't," said Frank. "I typed my password so

6

that the computer will know it's really me. But the password didn't appear on the screen so that nosy people like you can't find out what it is."

"Why do you need a password?" asked Joe. "Does this Jim Lerner guy keep state secrets on his computer or something?"

Frank shrugged. "Mostly it's so nobody else can read my electronic mail. And to keep unauthorized users off."

"Electronic mail?" asked Joe. "What's that?"

"You're a font of ignorance," said Frank. "Just keep watching."

More words flashed on the screen:

Hello, Frank Hardy.
　　You have visited the Cosmic Citadel BBS 5 times.
　　Your last visit was 6 days ago.
　　You have 59 minutes remaining today.
　　You have mail waiting!

"How does it know you have mail?" asked Joe. "Want me to go check the box?"

"Not that kind of mail!" said his brother in exasperation. "It means BBS mail. I'll show you."

There was a pause, and then the screen of the computer cleared. More words flowed onto the screen:

THE COSMIC CITADEL BBS
+==MENU OF OPTIONS==+

Type '?' for HELP

<C>hat with Sysop   <R>ead Messages
<E>lectronic Mail   <P>ost Messages
<G>ames On-line   <L>ist Files
<S>ystem Information   <U>pload Files
<B>BS Listings   <D>ownload Files

"Okay," said Frank. "You see where it says 'Electronic mail'? That means that if I type the letter *E*, Jim's computer will print my mail on the screen."

"Gotcha," said Joe. "Let's read your mail. Or am I not allowed to see it? Remember, I don't have a password."

"I'll let you get by just this once," said Frank. "Then maybe we can get you a password of your own."

"Uh-uh," said Joe. "I want nothing to do with computers. Nothing at all."

"Suit yourself," said Frank. He typed *E*, then pressed the key marked Enter. More words spewed across the screen:

You have 1 letter waiting.

FROM: Jim Lerner (Sysop)
TO: Frank Hardy
SUBJECT: How's It Going?
Hey, Frank, just wanted to let you know that the PD program you asked for is in the D/L section. Glad to hear you've got that AT clone up and

running, with that 4800 baud modem. Bet that 386 processor really screams! Let me know when you get the VGA board. BTW we ought to get together soon. I can introduce you to Becky and meet that mysterious brother of yours. <grin> Best, Jim

Joe squinted at the screen, muttering to himself as he tried to read the electronic letter. "Doesn't this guy know English?" he asked. "I don't understand half of what he says here. And what's this business about your 'mysterious brother'?"

"I've mentioned your name to him a few times," said Frank. "And he's mentioned his girlfriend, Becky, a few times. So he always jokes about my mysterious brother that he's never met, and I always joke about his mysterious girlfriend, who I've never met."

"Why don't you pick up the phone and talk to the guy?" asked Joe. "Ask him if he wants to play some softball. Why do you have to leave him these—these electronic messages?"

"Because it's more fun to do it that way," said Frank. "Besides, I don't even know if he's home."

"Can you find out?" Joe asked. "I want to get out of here and toss a ball around."

"I can put his computer into chat mode," said Frank. He typed a command that caused the menu of options to reappear. He pointed at the line that read <C>hat with Sysop.

"What does that do?" said Joe.

"It causes a bell to ring on his computer system," explained Frank. "If he's home, he'll hear it and come over to the computer, and we can type messages back and forth."

"*Why can't you just pick up the phone and talk?*" shouted Joe, suddenly exasperated by his brother's insistence at doing everything by computer.

"Because it isn't done that way!" Frank shouted back, reaching for the keyboard to type a *C*.

Before he reached it, however, an unexpected message appeared on the computer screen:

Sysop Jim Lerner would like to chat with you. Please stand by.

"Well, well," said Frank, staring at the screen. "Jim *is* home. And he wants to talk to us. He put the computer into chat mode himself."

Joe stared grumpily at his brother. "Well, if you two are just going to type at each other for the next hour, I'm going to grab a softball and see if I can find somebody who wants to play. Maybe Chet Morton's home."

"Hang on a second," said Frank. "Jim's starting to type something. Maybe he's got some interesting news."

"Oh, boy," said Joe unenthusiastically. "Maybe he's got a new 2001 baud 747 processor to show you."

"Nice to see that you're picking up the jargon," said Frank sarcastically.

10

Letters began appearing on the video display one at a time, as though being pecked out slowly by a two-finger typist. The first word to appear was:

HELP!!

Frank sat bolt upright in his chair. "Something's wrong," he said.

"Is this a joke?" asked Joe. "Grab the phone and talk to him."

"I can't," said Frank. "It's attached to a modem at his end, too. All we'll hear is electronic noise. We have to let him type."

"That'll take forever," said Joe. "It's obvious this guy's never taken a typing class."

More words appeared, with painful slowness, on the screen. The brothers hovered in front of the computer. All they could do was watch as Jim finished typing his message. Finally it was complete. It read:

HELP!! I THINK I'M DYING!! COME TO MY HOUSE IMMEDIAAZZCV

2 "ShE IS ILL"

"Where's this guy's house?" asked Joe, staring at the urgent message on the computer screen. "How fast can we get there?"

"About five blocks away," said Frank. "The big white house near the corner of Danville and Shea."

"Let's go!" said Joe. "We'd better get moving! We'll take the van."

"No," said Frank. "I'll drive the van over to Jim's, you call the cops and tell them to meet me there. Then you can follow on foot."

"Right," said Joe. "How do I disconnect this phone from the—the modem?"

"Use the phone in your room," said Frank. "It's a different line. I don't want to break the connection with Jim. If I shut down the link to his computer, there's no way we can get back in contact."

Frank dashed down the stairs and out the front door as Joe headed for his room. Once outside, Frank clambered into the modified police van that he shared with his brother and gunned the engine to life. The tires squealed as he pulled into the street.

About a minute and a half later he screeched to a halt in front of Jim Lerner's house. Frank ran up the front walk and knocked loudly on the door.

There was no answer. He tried the handle, and it turned easily. When he pushed on the door, it popped open.

Frank peered inside. The front hallway was dark, and the living room beyond it appeared deserted. There seemed to be no one at home.

"Hello?" Frank shouted. His voice echoed in the silence, but no one answered. Taking a deep breath, Frank stepped inside.

He had never been in Jim Lerner's house before. The living room was neatly kept and filled with well-padded, old-fashioned furniture. The morning newspaper was lying in several pieces on the coffee table, as though someone had been reading it not long before.

"Anybody home?" said Frank, peering into the hallway on the other side of the living room. The hallway was dark. So were the two rooms leading off it, which appeared to be a kitchen and a small dining room. Frank quickly poked his head inside each and looked around, but there was no sign of Jim.

At the end of the hallway was a flight of stairs. A dim light trickled down from somewhere above.

"Jim?" said Frank, running toward the stairs. "You up there?"

He raced up the steps, taking them two at a time. The light was coming from an open door at the end of another long hallway. Frank ran to the door and looked inside.

It was an ordinary-looking teenager's bedroom, with posters of rock singers on the wall, a model of a spaceship hanging from the ceiling, and magazines and notebooks scattered on the floor. A single bed with blue sheets and a wooden frame was tucked in one corner. Next to the bed was a bureau with one drawer open and a couple of socks hanging out.

On the far side of the room, a skinny young man of about seventeen with wavy brown hair, dressed in khaki pants and a light blue shirt, sat on a small wooden chair in front of a wooden table. He was slumped forward, his head propped against the side of the keyboard of a computer much like the one Frank had been using in his room, although Frank didn't recognize the brand name, Workwell. His right hand, its fingers tightly clenched, lay across the computer's keyboard, while his left hand was in his lap. On the screen of the computer was a set of messages just like the ones that had just flashed across Frank's computer screen.

14

"Jim!" shouted Frank, startled by the sight of his friend. "What's wrong?"

There was no response. Frank rushed across the room and grabbed his friend by the shoulders, but his body was limp and Jim collapsed, unconscious, into Frank's arms. Frank picked him up and moved him to the nearby bed.

Frank felt for Jim's pulse. It was weak. Jim's right hand was still clenched tightly. Frank gently loosened the fingers, and a small, ragged slip of paper fell out, looking like something that Jim had torn from a larger sheet.

Frank picked it up. On one side was a short message printed in the kind of type called dot matrix, with each letter made up of tiny dots of ink. It read:

ShE IS ILL

Frank glanced at the paper for a moment, then tucked it into his shirt pocket. He had no idea what the message meant, but he could worry about that later. Looking at Jim lying on the bed, he wondered how long it would take the police to arrive. After a few more minutes of worrying and wondering, he heard the front door open and his brother's voice call, "Frank? Are you in here?"

"Upstairs!" Frank shouted. "Get up here fast!"

Seconds later he heard Joe bounding up the stairs. He burst into the room, panting for breath.

"I ran all the way over here," he gasped. Then he

15

looked down at the bed. "Is that Jim? What happened to him?"

"I can't tell," said Frank. "He's still alive, but he doesn't look like he's in very good shape."

"Any injuries?" asked Joe. "See any blood or anything?"

"No," said Frank. "Are the police on the way?"

"I think that's them now," said Joe. The sound of sirens rising and falling came through the open window of the bedroom.

Within another minute a rescue squad vehicle veered up to the curb next to the Hardy's van. A police car pulled up next. Joe went downstairs to show them up to the bedroom where Frank waited.

The paramedics swarmed around Jim's bed, taking his vital signs, while Frank tried to explain what had happened. A pair of police officers stood in the door, watching the action and staying out of the way.

Jim was still unconscious as the medics carried him downstairs on a stretcher and placed him in the ambulance that was waiting by the curb. The Hardys and the police officers watched anxiously as the medics strapped him inside.

Frank turned to one of the medics, who had jumped out of the back of the ambulance. "Do you have any idea what's wrong with him?" he asked.

"It's hard to tell," he said. "But at his age it's not likely to be a heart attack or a stroke."

"So what's left?" Frank asked.

"If I had to guess," the medic replied, "I'd say he was poisoned."

"Poisoned!" said Joe. "You mean somebody tried to kill him?"

"I didn't say that," the medic said. "Maybe it was an accident. Maybe he ate something he shouldn't have or took the wrong medicine. It's up to the police to decide how it happened. Now we'd better get him to the hospital."

Joe looked at his brother as the ambulance pulled away, its siren wailing. "Do you think this was an accident? Food poisoning or something?"

"I don't know," said Frank. "If that's all it was, why did he say that he was dying?"

"Maybe he was exaggerating," said Joe. "Maybe he felt so sick he *thought* he was dying."

"No," said Frank. "Jim's not like that. He never makes a big deal out of things."

"Maybe we should take a look around Jim's house," Joe suggested. "See if we can find signs of foul play."

"No, you don't," said one of the police officers, who had overheard the conversation. "We've got everything under control here. We'll be in touch with the victim's family, and we'll investigate the scene. You boys just get on home now."

"But, Officer," said Joe Hardy. "We're detectives. It's okay."

"Right," said the policeman. "And I'm an astronaut. See you on Mars, boys. 'Bye!"

17

"Come on, Joe," said Frank, tugging his brother toward the Hardy van. "Aunt Gertrude's roast beef is probably getting cold."

Joe gave the policeman a dirty look. "I think I've lost my appetite," he growled.

"So," said Joe the next morning between forkfuls of scrambled eggs. "When do we get started on the Lerner case?"

"What case?" replied Frank from across the breakfast table. "You heard that cop last night. The police have the whole thing under control."

"I know what they said," answered Joe. "But Jim Lerner is your friend. I'd think you'd be a little more interested in finding out what happened to him."

"I am." Frank smiled. "Maybe I've already called Jim's mom but got no answer. So maybe now I'm thinking about giving his girlfriend, Becky, a call this morning to see what she knows about Jim's, ah, accident."

"Attaboy!" said Joe enthusiastically. "I'll rev up the van so we can hit the road and get down to some serious detective work."

"Slow down!" said Frank. "Let me call Becky first. Remember, this whole thing could still turn out to be an accident. Then there won't be any case to solve."

"Do you have Becky's phone number?" asked Joe. "Or do you want me to hand you the phone book?"

"Jim put her number on the bulletin board," said Frank, "so that users could call her in case they had problems logging on, downloading files, that kind of thing. I think I saved her number on my computer." He pushed himself away from the table. "Come on. Let's take a look."

"Oh, no!" groaned Joe. "Not the computer again! I thought we were going to do some real detective work, not this nerd stuff."

Frank made a face. "Ease up," he said. "Computers can be fun. They're not just for nerds."

"You sound like Phil Cohen," said Joe. "I don't want to do anything on a computer that doesn't involve a joystick."

"Hmm," said Frank. "We'll see about that. Meanwhile, let's find Becky's number."

Upstairs, Frank turned on the computer and typed in a series of commands. A flood of bright green characters appeared on the screen. Frank watched the display intently until he saw what he was looking for, then pressed down on a pair of keys to make the words on the display freeze in place.

"Here's Becky's number," he said. "Write it down."

Joe pointed at the modem. "Why don't you just ask the computer to call it?"

"It's not that simple," said Frank. "We'll have to do it the old-fashioned way, with our fingers."

"Ah," said Joe with a smile. "My area of expertise! Want me to do it?"

"No," said Frank. "I'd better make the call. I'm

Jim's friend, and Becky's probably pretty upset about what happened to him yesterday."

Frank picked up the phone and punched out the number. It rang twice, then a woman—apparently Becky's mother—answered the phone. Frank asked for Becky North.

"She can't come to the phone right now," the woman told him. "She's had some rather bad news."

"I know," said Frank. "It was about her boyfriend, right? I'm a friend of Jim's. I was there when they took him to the hospital."

"Oh," said the mother. "Then perhaps she would like to talk to you. Hold on for a moment."

The woman put the phone down with a clunk. Frank could hear voices in the distance, then someone picked up the phone and said in a soft voice, "Hello?"

"Becky?" Frank said. "This is Frank Hardy. I know your boyfriend, Jim, from school. I was there last night when he was, ah, taken sick."

"Oh," she said, sounding distraught. "Do you know what happened?"

"Not exactly," said Frank. "I was hoping you could tell me. Jim was unconscious when I got there."

"I don't have any details," said Becky. "I was going to go to the hospital this afternoon. All I know is that Jim is still unconscious and the doctors aren't sure why."

Frank explained that he had been chatting with Jim over the BBS when his mysterious ailment had struck. Becky's voice suddenly became more excited.

"Maybe you should talk to Jim's mother," she said. "She's really upset. She was at the hospital all night, but maybe she's home now. I'm sure she'd want to know everything that you know about what happened to Jim."

"Okay," said Frank. "I'll go over there now. Why don't you meet me there? You can introduce me to Jim's mother."

"I'll be there in a half hour," said Becky.

"Well?" said Joe when Frank hung up. "Are we going to do some detective work?"

"Looks that way," said Frank. "We're going back to the scene of the crime. If there was one."

A half hour later Frank and Joe turned the corner of Danville and Shea and angled into a parking place in front of Jim Lerner's big white house. A small blue car that had not been there the night before was in front of the house.

"That must be Becky's car," said Frank. "Guess she beat us here."

"Right," said Joe, suddenly frowning. "And who do you suppose that is?"

"Huh?" said Frank. "Who are you talking about?"

"There," said Joe, pointing at the side of the Lerner house.

21

Barely visible behind a tall tree in the yard, a darkly dressed figure was lowering himself out of Jim Lerner's open bedroom window and onto an aluminum ladder. He was holding a small box in one hand.

"Someone's robbing Jim's house!" Joe cried.

3 Password to Mystery

Joe leapt out of the van ahead of Frank and ran toward the burglar sneaking out of Jim Lerner's bedroom.

The burglar, a dark-haired man in his twenties wearing black jeans and a dark pullover sweater, looked down to see Joe running straight toward him. Panicking, he jumped down the rest of the way to the ground, staggered for a moment from the impact, then ran toward the back-yard.

"Hey, you!" shouted Joe, gaining quickly on the intruder. "What do you think you're doing?"

Glancing briefly at Joe, the burglar doubled his speed, racing toward the fence that lined the Lerners' backyard. A wooden rake, lying sideways across the lawn, didn't catch his attention. He stumbled across it and sprawled headlong into the grass.

Taking advantage of the burglar's misstep, Joe launched himself at the fallen figure in an attempt to pin him to the ground. But the burglar was quicker than Joe had anticipated. He rolled out of the way, and Joe landed on solid ground.

"Oof!" cried Joe, stunned by the sudden impact.

"What's going on?" cried Frank, rounding the side of the house in pursuit of his brother.

At the sound of Frank's voice, the burglar leapt to his feet and began running again.

"Hey!" shouted Joe, stumbling back to his feet. He was too late, though. By the time Joe was once again in pursuit, the burglar was hoisting himself over the fence into the backyard of the next house.

Joe and Frank reached the fence simultaneously, but the burglar was halfway to the next street and disappearing fast.

"Did you get a look at him?" Frank asked. "All I saw was the back of his head."

"Yeah, I saw him," said Joe. "I didn't recognize him, but I'll know him if I see him again."

"Do you see what I see?" said Frank, looking back in the direction from which they had come. "I think our friend dropped the box he was carrying."

A small, red cardboard box was lying on the grass in the middle of the backyard. Joe rushed over and picked it up.

"What is it?" said Frank.

Joe held the box up so that Frank could see it. On one side "DS/DD Floppy Disks/Package of Ten" was written.

"Computer disks!" cried Frank. "And I bet that they're from Jim's computer!" He opened the box briefly and looked inside. "Only two disks in here, though."

Suddenly the back door of the Lerner house opened and a stout woman of about forty looked out. She was dressed in a faded blue bathrobe and wore floppy slippers on her feet. Her hair was tousled and uncombed, and there were deep rings beneath her eyes. "What's going on out here?" she said. "What's all this noise?"

"Oh, hello," said Frank sheepishly. "You must be Mrs. Lerner. My name's Frank Hardy."

"Oh, yes," the woman said. "Becky was just telling me about you. What are you doing back here?"

Frank decided against telling Jim's mother about the burglar, as she had enough to worry about at the moment. "Uh, my brother Joe and I thought we saw something lying in the backyard," said Frank to Mrs. Lerner, pointing to the box of floppy disks that Joe was holding. "Do these look like something that might belong to Jim?"

"I don't know," she said. Her voice sounded tired. "They might be. He has so many computer things, I have trouble keeping track."

She held the screen door open for the brothers to

25

enter. As he stepped past her, Frank saw that her eyes were red and rimmed with tears. She had been crying.

Mrs. Lerner led the Hardys through the kitchen and into the living room they had seen the evening before. Sitting on the sofa, sipping from a cup of tea perched on the edge of the coffee table, was a pretty, dark-haired girl of sixteen or seventeen, wearing a blue knit dress cinched at the waist with a wide leather belt. She had a round face and large eyes. Her hair was pinned back from her forehead with a tortoiseshell comb but fell down around her neck in back. She rose as Frank and Joe entered the room and nodded to them.

"You must be Becky," said Frank. "I'm Frank Hardy. This is my brother, Joe."

"Glad to meet you," said Becky. "I remembered your name after I talked to you on the phone. I've seen your messages on Jim's bulletin board. You and your brother are detectives, aren't you?"

"Well, yeah," said Frank. "Amateur detectives. We've solved a few cases around the Bayport area."

Mrs. Lerner looked at the Hardys with new interest. "Detectives?" she said. "Maybe—maybe you can help find out what happened to my—to my son."

"We're really sorry about what happened to Jim," said Frank to Mrs. Lerner. "I was chatting with him on the computer last night when he went unconscious."

26

"Did he say what had happened?" asked Mrs. Lerner. "The doctors don't seem to know what's wrong."

"All he said was—" Frank began, then hesitated. "Well, he said that he was dying. I don't know why he said that. He was probably just sick—and upset."

Mrs. Lerner looked distraught. "I'm sure he didn't know what he was saying. And I'm—I'm sure he'll be okay." She looked around the room distractedly. "I'm afraid I have to get ready for work. Why don't you young people talk with one another for a moment?" Then she left the room.

Frank and Joe settled down into a pair of armchairs across from Becky. "Let me ask you something," said Frank. "Do you know if anybody might have wanted to hurt your boyfriend?"

"Are you being detectives now?" she asked, frowning. "Do *you* think somebody tried to hurt Jim?"

"One of the medics last night said it looked like Jim might have been poisoned," said Joe. "It might just be food poisoning or something. We won't know until the doctors give Mrs. Lerner their report."

"Well," said Becky, "I can't imagine why anybody would do such a thing to him. Jim's very popular. I don't know anybody who dislikes him."

Joe held up the box of floppy disks. "Do you know if these belong to him?"

27

She gave the box a puzzled look. "Maybe," she said. "That's the brand of disks he used. Where did you get those?"

In a quiet voice Joe told her about the burglar in the backyard. Becky looked shocked.

"I—I was sitting in here with Mrs. Lerner!" she said. "Do you mean to tell me that somebody was breaking into the house at the same time?"

"Yep," said Joe. "He must have slipped in and out of Jim's room without your knowing it. And he took these."

He handed her the box. She opened the lid and reached inside.

She took the two disks out and examined them. One was labeled Lerner/BBS/Executables and the other Lerner/BBS/Data.

"These are Jim's BBS disks," Becky concluded. "This one has the BBS program on it, and the other has the messages and other files."

Joe looked at Frank. "Why would that guy want to take them?"

"Maybe there's something important on them," said Frank. He turned back to Becky. "Can we take a closer look at those disks? On Jim's computer?"

"Sure," said Becky. "I'll take you up to his room."

Jim Lerner's bedroom was exactly as they had left it the evening before, except that someone had turned off the computer. The window was open. Frank stepped over to it and looked down at the aluminum ladder the burglar had used to get through the window.

Becky stood beside him and followed his gaze. "That's Mrs. Lerner's ladder." She gulped, still frightened by the robbery. "The burglar must have taken it from the backyard."

"It's not a good idea to leave ladders lying around," said Joe. "It's practically inviting somebody to climb in your window. I think I'll run downstairs and put that ladder away. Don't start without me." In ten minutes he was back.

Becky took a deep breath and sat down in front of the computer. She slid the small, square floppy disks into two slots under the computer's video monitor. Then she turned the computer on. The computer made a rattling, humming sound, as if it were shaking itself awake after a night's sleep.

Joe looked sheepishly at Frank. "I don't want to sound dumb or anything," he said, "but would somebody mind explaining to me just what a floppy disk does?"

"It's kind of like recording tape," said Frank, "except that it's round and flat instead of long and skinny."

"And it records computer data instead of music," added Becky.

"Computer data?" asked Joe.

"Like programs and messages and stuff," said Frank.

Becky pointed at the two narrow slots under the computer's video display. "These are the disk drives. I put the disks into the drives so that the computer can 'read' them, the way that you'd put a tape cassette into a tape recorder."

"Oh," said Joe, nodding his head slightly.

"Looks like you're going to learn something about computers whether you want to or not," said Frank, a smile on his lips.

"I promise to forget every bit of it as soon as I get a chance," said Joe. "So what kind of, uh, computer data is on those disks?"

Becky pointed at the disk drives. "The first disk contains Jim's BBS program. That's the set of electronic instructions that tells the computer how to run the BBS."

"Doesn't the computer already know how to do that?" asked Joe. "I thought computers were smarter than we are."

"Not quite," said Becky. "Actually, the computer is a complete idiot until I put the program in it. The program makes it smarter, in a way, but not as smart as we are."

"Well," Frank said, laughing, "maybe smarter than Joe here."

"I'll pretend I didn't hear that," said Joe. "So if the BBS program is on the first disk, what's on the second?"

"That's where Jim keeps all the files relating to the BBS," said Becky.

"Files?" asked Joe.

"It's the way in which computers store useful information on the disk," said Becky. "Like the electronic mail and all the other things you can read when you're logged on to the BBS. You can ask the computer to give you a directory—a list of names —of all the files on the disk."

"Could some of that information be worth stealing?" asked Frank.

"I can't imagine why," said Becky. "I mean, some of it was private mail but nothing important. Not important enough to steal, anyway."

"Apparently the burglar thought it was," said Joe.

The computer made a beeping sound to indicate that the BBS program was now up and running. The words *COSMIC CITADEL BBS* appeared on the screen in big block letters.

"This is what's on the first disk," said Becky. "The BBS program itself."

"I don't see why the burglar would have wanted to steal that," said Joe.

"Jim would have *given* him a copy if he'd asked," said Becky. "Jim wrote this program himself. He was always giving it away. He never charged anybody for it."

"Then maybe what the burglar was looking for was on the second disk," said Frank. "Can we see what's on it?"

"That depends," said Becky.

"On what?" asked Joe.

"On your security level," she replied.

"Huh?" said Frank and Joe simultaneously.

"Jim was very cautious about who was allowed to read what on the BBS," Becky explained. "Most sysops are. Therefore he gave everybody a security level between one and ten that determined how much they could see. When a new user joined the BBS, he or she received a security level of one. That allowed them to read the public messages that had been left for everyone to see and the electronic mail that was addressed to them. After a while Jim would boost users to a higher level if they seemed trustworthy. That allowed them to read special higher security messages. As the co-sysop, I have a security level of nine, which lets me read everything except private electronic mail. Jim, of course, gave himself a security level of ten, which lets him read everything."

"Then Jim can read other people's mail?" Frank asked.

"He *could*," Becky said, "but he never would. He's much too honest for that. He believes that the mail on his board is private and that it's wrong to read it unless it's addressed to him. Jim's a real straight-arrow guy."

"So how can we read the stuff that's on the other disk?" asked Joe.

"I can sign on to the BBS now and read everything except the private electronic mail," said Becky. "I'm afraid that we could read that only if Jim were here. My security level isn't high enough."

"How does the BBS know what your security level is?" asked Frank.

"Jim keeps that information on the disk," Becky

said. "When I sign on, the BBS will read my security level off the disk."

"Then why don't you sign on under Jim's name?" asked Joe. "If the board thinks that you're Jim, maybe it'll give you Jim's security level."

Becky shook her head. "It won't work. The board would ask for my password. If I didn't give it Jim's password, it wouldn't let me sign on under his name."

Joe shook his head, a baffled look on his face. "Well, don't you know Jim's password?"

"Of course not!" Becky said, an expression of horror in her eyes. "Passwords are sacred to Jim! He would never tell me his password or ask me for mine!"

"And if we don't know his password," said Frank in frustration, "we can't read the private electronic mail. Do you have a funny feeling, Joe, that the electronic mail is *exactly* what the burglar was after?"

"Uh-huh," said Joe, tapping the monitor in thought. "Listen, Becky, is there some other way to look at the information on that disk—without using the BBS program?"

"Sure," said Becky. "Jim has some disk editor programs that let you look at the information just as it's stored on the disk, without going through the BBS—but it wouldn't do any good."

"Why not?" Frank asked.

"Because Jim encrypted all of the data on the disk."

"Encrypted?" Joe repeated.

"Put it into a kind of code," said Becky. "Like a secret message. There's no way to decode it unless you know the secret key."

"Let me guess," said Frank. "Jim's the only one who knows the key."

"I'm afraid so," Becky confirmed.

"Then the only way to read it is by finding out Jim's password," said Joe. "Could he have written it down somewhere?"

"He might have," said Becky. "But I wouldn't know where to begin looking."

"Wait a minute!" said Frank, snapping his fingers. "When I found Jim unconscious last night, he had a piece of paper clutched in his hand. The words ShE IS ILL were printed on it."

"Maybe that's his password!" cried Joe.

Becky looked puzzled. "I suppose it's possible. Here. Let me give it a try."

She pressed a key on the computer, and it prompted her to type a name. She typed *Jim Lerner*. Then, when it asked her for a password, she typed SHE IS ILL.

The computer beeped. "Invalid password," it said.

"I guess that wasn't it," said Becky.

"Hold on," said Frank. "On the piece of paper the *H* in the word *she* was in lowercase instead of uppercase. Would that make a difference?"

Becky shook her head. "No. The BBS converts all the characters in the password into capital letters when you type. It wouldn't make any difference at all."

The three stared at the computer in frustration. Both of the Hardys were aware that whatever the burglar had been looking for was somewhere on the second disk—and they couldn't get to it.

Suddenly Mrs. Lerner appeared in the doorway, moving unsteadily. Her face was pale, frozen. "What's wrong, Mrs. Lerner?" asked Becky.

"It's Jim," she said, her voice shaking. "The doctor just called from the hospital. He wants to see me immediately.

"He says Jim is dying!"

4 Designer Poison

Becky stood and placed her arm around Mrs. Lerner's shoulders.

"Come on," said Frank. "We'll drive you to the hospital."

Jim's mother nodded her head in thanks.

"I'll come, too," said Becky. "I'm sure the doctor's wrong. Jim will be okay, you'll see."

Fifteen minutes later Frank pulled up the Hardy van at the entrance to Bayport General Hospital and paused while Mrs. Lerner and Becky went inside. By the time Frank and Joe had parked the van and found their way to the floor Jim's room was on, it was obvious that the doctor had already talked to Mrs. Lerner about her son. Jim's mother was sitting in a corner of the waiting area, silently crying. Becky sat next to her, blowing her nose into a handkerchief, her eyes rimmed with tears.

Frank and Joe sat next to Becky, waiting for her to finish crying.

"Mrs. Lerner was right," said Becky between sniffles. "Jim *is* dying!"

"What's the matter?" asked Frank. "Did they say what had happened to him?"

"He was poisoned," she said. "They don't know how or why. There was a policeman here investigating."

"A policeman?" asked Joe. "Where?"

"Over there," she said, pointing to a uniformed officer talking with a doctor.

"That's Con Riley," Frank said. "We know him."

"Excuse us for a second, Becky," said Joe, rising to his feet. "We're going to talk to this guy."

As the Hardys approached, Officer Riley turned to look at them. "Well, if it isn't Frank and Joe. I've been looking for you boys."

"You know our phone number, Con," said Frank. "Call us whenever you need us."

"The desk sarge tells me it was you guys who called in to report this Jim Lerner thing last night," Con said. "Is that right?"

"That's right," said Joe.

"Which of you was the first on the scene?" asked Con.

"I was," said Frank. "I got to the house while Joe was calling in the troops. Jim was already unconscious. I guess he never woke up."

37

"No," said Con.

"Is there any hope for him?" asked Joe.

"Hard to say," said Con. "Maybe if—"

"Officer," interrupted a woman's voice. The Hardys turned to see Mrs. Lerner. "Officer, I want you and the doctor to tell these boys the same things you told me about what happened to Jim."

"Well, ma'am," said Con, "I'm not sure we should. We're not even handing out that information to the newspapers quite yet."

"Please," said Mrs. Lerner. "I think they can help find out what happened to my son. I'm going back to the waiting area to sit with Becky."

Con sighed, then shrugged at the Hardys. "Well, I guess it couldn't hurt to have you on our side as long as we've got Mrs. Lerner's say-so. Come on, boys. I'll have Dr. Madison talk to you."

The police officer led the Hardys to the end of the hospital hallway, where a doctor in a white lab coat was talking to a nurse. When the doctor finished, Con introduced him to the Hardys as Dr. Herbert Madison. He was a plump, silver-haired man in his sixties with a reddish complexion. He nodded to the Hardys and led them into a small office with four chairs.

"Frank and Joe are our local boy-wonder detectives," said Con as the group of four settled down onto the hard wooden chairs. "Mrs. Lerner wants you to brief them on Jim's condition, in case they can help us on this case."

"I'm glad to meet you, boys," said Dr. Madison, shaking hands with the Hardys. "I'd better give you a little background on myself first, so you'll understand how I diagnosed what's wrong with Jim. I'm afraid most doctors would have been quite baffled by his condition. It's fortunate that I was working here in Bayport and could be called in on the case, though I'm not sure it's going to do the Lerner boy much good.

"I worked in a government-operated research hospital until about two years ago, when I retired to a private practice here in Bayport. I was involved in toxin research. That's why Jim's doctor got hold of me when he suspected poisoning. When I examined the young man, I realized that what he had been exposed to was not run-of-the-mill, but one of the new experimental toxins that I'd been studying before I came here."

"Experimental toxins?" said Joe. "I thought a poison was a poison."

"Far from it," said Dr. Madison. "The darker side of our new medical technologies is that they can be used to create effective ways to end lives as well as to save them. We can now use genetic engineering techniques to tailor living organisms—bacteria and viruses—to attack the human body in very precise and terrifying ways. The poison that was used on Jim is a kind of 'designer poison,' intended to kill an individual slowly over a period of days while leaving him in a coma."

39

"How much longer does he have?" asked Frank.

"Judging by his vital signs, about a week, I'd say," replied the doctor.

"Is there any cure?" asked Joe. "An antidote?"

"Quite possibly," said the doctor. "But only the person or persons who designed the poison would know how to design the antidote. But if we don't know who poisoned him, we don't know where to find the antidote."

"This doesn't sound like an accident," said Frank.

"It isn't," said Con. "It's attempted murder. And if we don't find that antidote, it'll be first-degree murder."

"Then we've got to find the poisoner," said Joe, "to save Jim Lerner's life."

"That's about the size of it," said Con.

"Do you have any idea who did the poisoning?" Frank asked Con.

"No," he said. "I was hoping you boys might have some suggestions. You know the Lerner boy, after all."

"Actually," said Joe, "I never met him. Not while he was conscious, anyway."

"And I didn't know him that well," said Frank. "I had a couple of classes with him in school, and we exchanged some electronic mail."

"Electronic mail?" asked Con.

"Don't ask," Joe advised.

"You'd be better off talking with his girlfriend,

Becky," said Frank. "She's sitting in the waiting area with Jim's mother."

"Thanks for the tip," said Con. "If you kids learn anything, be sure and let me know."

"Have we ever kept any clues from you, Con?" Joe asked innocently.

"Do you want an itemized list?" Con asked in return.

"Thanks for the briefing, Dr. Madison," said Frank.

"Happy to help, boys," said the doctor.

The Hardys rejoined Becky and Mrs. Lerner. Becky thanked the brothers again for driving Mrs. Lerner and herself to the hospital but added that they would be staying for several more hours and would take a taxi home later.

Frank and Joe said goodbye and left. Outside the hospital Joe turned to Frank and gave him a questioning look. "What now?" he asked.

"I still think the first place to look is on those computer disks," Frank said. "Good thing I took them when we left Jim's place."

"So they're in the van?" Joe asked.

"Right," said Frank. "Now we ought to have somebody take a look at them, somebody who knows a lot about computers."

"Who did you have in mind?" asked Joe.

"I don't know," said Frank. "It would have to be a real computer expert, like—"

"Phil Cohen," said Joe.

41

"Right," said Frank. "Phil's helped us out on cases before. And he probably knows more about computers than most professional programmers."

Joe groaned. "I just told Phil yesterday that I didn't need to know anything about computers to help with my detective work. Now he's going to make me eat my words."

"Enjoy the meal," said Frank, heading for the Hardy van. "We might not have time for lunch."

Phil Cohen lived a few blocks from the intersection where Jim Lerner resided. His "workshop," as he liked to call it, was located in a garage next to the house. The Hardys parked in front of the garage and rapped loudly on the door. Phil poked his head out and laughed when he saw Joe standing there.

"Aha!" he cried. "So you took me up on my offer, huh? Got tired of tossing that ball around and decided to enter the computer age?"

"Uh, not quite," said Joe. "Frank and I are on a case, and we think you might be able to give us a hand."

"Hey, guys!" said Phil. "I'm always willing to help. Come on in."

Phil led the brothers inside the garage and into his inner sanctum. At first glance his laboratory looked like a random collection of electronic and other kinds of scientific junk. On closer examination, though, the shelves and tabletops filled with electronic equipment, scientific supplies, and carefully arranged experiments turned out to have a bizarre logic of their own. Phil had arranged all the equipment so that everything he needed was close at hand and ready to be used. But Joe doubted that anyone but Phil could have located anything in the place.

"So what's up?" he asked. "How can I help you out?"

Frank showed him the disks. "Can you tell us what's on these disks? Especially this one?"

"I don't see why not," he said. "Why do you need to know?"

Frank told him about Jim Lerner's poisoning and the burglar they had seen climbing out of his bedroom. "We think what he wanted was on the second disk, the one labeled Lerner/BBS/Data. He's got it rigged so nobody can read it without the right password, but we figured if anybody could get past an electronic roadblock, it was you."

"Well," said Phil, taking the disks in hand, "you're probably right on that count. But it could take time."

"How much time?" asked Joe.

"That depends on how tightly he's got the disk protected," said Phil. "It might take minutes. Or it might take weeks."

"We don't *have* weeks," Frank pointed out. "If we don't crack this case in exactly *one* week, Jim'll be dead."

"Then I'll give it my best shot," said Phil. "Let's take a closer look at these disks."

He turned to a microcomputer on a wooden shelf

behind him and popped the disks into the disk drives as Becky had done earlier. Then he turned the computer on.

"A BBS program, huh?" said Phil. "I'd heard about Jim Lerner's BBS, but I never logged on. He's supposed to be a really sharp programmer. I can't wait to take a look at his program."

"Don't enjoy it *too* much," said Joe. "We've got a case to solve here."

"Relax," said Phil. "I may have to analyze the program to find out how he's got the data stored. It'll be both work and play for me." He tapped a few keys on the computer's keyboard, studying the information that appeared on the computer screen. "Yeah, he's got a lot of stuff on these disks. Let's take a closer look at the second disk."

He pulled out the first disk, then inserted the other disk in one of the drives. He typed something and pressed Enter. The computer rattled and hummed, and the screen filled with numbers and characters.

"Uh-oh," said Phil.

"What's wrong?" asked Frank.

"The stuff you're looking at on the screen here is the data on the second disk," said Phil.

"It looks like gibberish," said Joe.

"That's exactly what it is," said Phil, poking some more keys. Screen after screen of nonsense characters appeared on the display. "He's got this stuff encoded, right?"

"His girlfriend, Becky, said he had it encrypted," said Frank.

"That explains it," said Phil. "This may be tougher than I thought. If he's using a really heavy encryption scheme on this, it may be impossible to break the code."

"Impossible?" Joe asked. "I thought you could work miracles on these machines."

"There are miracles and there are miracles," said Phil. "Look, guys, I can analyze Jim's program to see what makes it tick, and maybe I can get it to decode these messages for me, but I can't guarantee any results. And I can't tell you how long it's going to take."

Frank and Joe exchanged glances. "Well, I guess that's the most we can ask," Frank said. "You work on these disks while Joe and I do our own detective work. Give us a call if you come up with something."

"I will," said Phil. "Believe me, I'll plug away on this night and day until I crack it. Or until it cracks me."

"Thanks, Phil," said Joe. He and his brother left the garage and reentered the van.

"Where to next?" said Joe.

"Home, I guess," said Frank. "We'll grab a quick lunch and do some clever detective-type thinking."

Frank drove the van back to their house. As they approached, they were surprised to see their aunt Gertrude standing in the front yard. She held a piece of paper in her hand. Her face was etched with lines, unmistakably worried.

"What's the matter, Aunt Gertrude?" Joe asked as he climbed out of the van.

"I just don't understand what gets into people," she said sharply. "Some—some *hooligan* left this on our front porch."

She handed the paper to Frank. On it was written a message in large block letters:

GIVE ME THE FLOPPY DISKS!
LEAVE THEM IN THE MAILBOX AT
3100 LYONS CIRCLE AT 2 P.M.
. . . OR YOUR LIVES ARE IN DANGER!!
—THE STALKER

5 Surprise Attack

"What's this about floppy disks?" growled Con Riley, standing in the Hardys' living room with the threatening note in his hand. "Why didn't you boys mention this to me this morning?"

"It, uh, must have slipped our minds," said Joe.

"These things *always* seem to slip your minds," Con retorted. "Is there anything else you've forgotten to mention to me?"

"Sorry, Con," said Joe. "It's a complicated case. I guess maybe we should have spent more time comparing notes this morning."

"Well, there's no time for that now," said Con. "This note says you're to have the disks in the mailbox at two P.M., and it's nearly one P.M. already. We'd better get a move on. You can fill me in on all these little details later—if they haven't slipped your minds again."

"What about the floppy disks?" asked Joe. "We left them at Phil Cohen's place."

"Leave them there," said Con. "They'll be safe. We don't want to give the real disks to this Stalker guy. They may be important clues. Besides, if I remember your friend Phil correctly, he's a real whiz kid. I wouldn't know what to do with the disks if I had them, but Phil just might."

"Then we did the right thing by taking them to Phil?" asked Frank.

"For once," said Con. "Okay, maybe you kids aren't so dumb. But try to keep me informed about how my case is proceeding, just for appearance's sake? The guys down at the squad room expect me to do a little work occasionally, you know."

"Right, Con," said Frank. "Always glad to help you out."

"Okay," Con said. "Now, what I want you two to do is to hop into that van of yours and drive over to 3100 Lyons Circle. Leave a couple of blank floppy disks in the box and hightail it out of there. Meanwhile, some of the boys and I will be watching the scene to see who picks up the disks."

"Do you know who lives at 3100 Lyons Circle?" asked Frank.

"No," said Con, "but we'll be finding out. And I hope he has a good alibi for the time that note was dropped on your porch."

Twenty minutes later Frank and Joe pulled their

van out of the driveway. They had phoned Phil Cohen to warn him to be extra careful with the disks and make copies of them in case something happened to the originals. Phil had informed them that although he had already copied the first disk, he hadn't been able to copy the second disk, the one with the messages on it. Jim Lerner had carefully prepared the disk so that no one could make a copy of it—except Jim himself.

"He sure was cautious about his bulletin board," Joe commented as Frank drove the van.

"Yeah," Frank agreed. "Too cautious. I guess he never figured that somebody might need to read that disk in order to save his life."

Number 3100 Lyons Circle was on the opposite side of Bayport from where the Hardys lived, and they arrived not long before the deadline given to them by the mysterious Stalker. A rural-delivery–style mailbox with no name on it stood at the roadside in front of a one-story house. While Frank kept the motor running, Joe exited the van, popped a small cardboard box inside the mailbox, and climbed back into the van. The cardboard box contained two blank floppy disks that Frank had bought for his own computer.

Frank drove the van around the corner, where they found Con Riley and a second police officer sitting inside an unmarked police car. Frank pulled the van to the curb, and the brothers got out and walked over to where the officers were sitting.

"What are you kids doing here?" Con snapped.

"I told you to leave the disks in that mailbox and then get out of the way."

"We did, Con," said Joe. "Now we want to see who picks up the disks."

"Nobody'll pick up the disks if you don't get your van out of here," said Con. "You'll scare 'em away."

"Okay, okay," said Frank. "We're going. Oh, by the way, did you find out who lives in that house?"

"Yeah," said Con. "Guy named Bob Eckerd. Claimed to know nothing about this floppy disk business. We'll be keeping an eye on him, though."

"Did he have an alibi for the time when the note was left on our porch?" asked Joe.

"Yeah, he had an alibi," said Con. "He was at work at the time. He's still at work. I talked to him on the phone."

There was a sudden squawking from the police radio in the car. Con leaned over and listened but didn't say anything.

"What a day!" he growled finally. "First this Stalker business, now they tell us that there's a fire in somebody's house. Well, the fire department can take care of that one. We've got to stake out this mailbox." He frowned at Frank and Joe. "Didn't I just tell you kids to get out of here?"

"We're going," said Frank, climbing back into the van. "Let us know if you catch anybody."

"Do you think this Bob Eckerd guy has anything to do with Jim's poisoning?" asked Joe once they were back in the van.

"No," said Frank as he revved up the engine.

50

"I'm sure he wouldn't have been stupid enough to give his own address to drop off the floppy disks at. That's like handing the police his identity on a silver platter."

"Hey, look." Joe pointed into the distance. "There's a cloud of smoke rising into the sky. Must be from the fire."

Frank gazed in the direction that Joe was pointing. Sure enough, a thin, greasy-looking cloud of smoke was drifting upward.

"Must be from that fire Con was talking about," Frank said. "Want to take a closer look?"

"Sure," said Joe. "Drive us in that direction."

"We're *already* driving in that direction," said Frank. "The fire is back toward our house."

Joe looked worried. "You don't suppose . . ."

"Calm down," said Frank. "It's not exactly in the same direction as our house. A few blocks away, I'd guess."

After they'd driven a few more blocks, Joe pointed out the window. "I can hear sirens from over there," he said. "I think we're almost at the fire."

As Frank drove around the corner, a fire truck cut in front of him and pulled to a stop at the curb. The smoke was rising from behind a two-story house in the middle of the block.

"Oh, no!" Frank cried. "I know whose house that is!"

"Right!" said Joe. "Phil Cohen's house!"

51

6 Digital Delights

The fire department was out in force. Three fire trucks blocked the street, and a dozen fire fighters were standing around with their hoses, though no water was coming out of them just then. Even as the Hardys watched, the cloud of black smoke began to disperse.

Phil himself was in the front yard, talking animatedly to a police officer. When he saw the Hardys get out of their van he waved at them and smiled broadly. "Frank, Joe! Over here!"

The brothers rushed to his side. "Are you okay?" Frank asked breathlessly.

"You don't look like somebody who just had his house almost burn down," Joe said.

"The fire wasn't in the house," Phil said. "It was in my lab." He pointed at the garage. There was a scorched spot around a window. Globs of white foam lay on the ground and around the edges of the window.

"What happened?" asked Frank. "One of your experiments catch on fire?"

"Not quite," said Phil. "I was in the workshop, and suddenly I saw flames outside the window. Fortunately, I've got a real state-of-the-art fire prevention system in the lab, in case one of my experiments does catch on fire. Anyway, the foam put the fire out before it could do much damage."

"Foam?" asked Joe.

"Special chemical foam," explained Phil. "For putting out fires. It sprays automatically when a fire's detected, kind of like a sprinkler system."

"And here we were worried about you," said Frank.

"Hey, guys," said Phil. "I can take care of myself. You know that. Anyway, I've got to tell the officer here about what happened. I'll be with you in a minute."

Frank and Joe wandered over to the garage to look around. The scorched window looked ominous, but when they stepped inside the workshop it seemed to be in its usual shape.

"Think it was an accident?" asked Frank.

"Nope," said Joe. "Too much of a coincidence. I think somebody set the fire deliberately."

Phil came inside a few minutes later. The first thing Frank and Joe wanted to know was if the disks were safe.

"Of course," said Phil. "You didn't think I'd let anything happen to them, did you?"

"Well," said Frank, "we didn't expect that you'd have to protect them with your life."

"Somebody must want to get rid of these disks real bad," Joe said.

"What do you mean?" asked Phil. Then a look of understanding came over his face. "You mean somebody set this fire because I had these disks?"

"Right," said Joe. "I'm not sure why they'd want to burn up the disks after going to all the trouble to steal them from Jim's bedroom. But I do know that this means it's more important than ever that we read what's on those disks."

Frank told Phil about the threatening note they had received. "We would have told you earlier, but we didn't have time," Frank said.

"How are you coming on cracking the secret code, Phil?" asked Joe.

"Not too good," Phil admitted. "This Lerner guy really knows what he's doing. I can't wait to talk to him about computers—if he ever wakes up."

"Wow," said Joe. "The ultimate compliment. Phil Cohen wants to ask Jim Lerner about computers."

"I didn't say I wanted to *ask* him anything," Phil pointed out. "But I figure I can tell him a thing or two. He's probably smart enough to understand."

54

"Listen, Phil," said Frank. "Are you sure you couldn't use some help on this job? Maybe if we turned it over to a whole team of computer experts or something?"

Phil looked indignant. "Are you suggesting I can't handle this?"

"No," Frank said quickly. "But maybe two heads would be better than one. After all, Jim Lerner's life may depend on breaking that code and reading that disk."

"I understand what you're saying," said Phil, "but it doesn't work that way. A team of cryptographers couldn't crack this kind of code using standard decoding techniques. Even the National Security Agency, where most of the expert cryptographers work, admits that codes like this are uncrackable if you don't know the key. What I'm doing is trying to understand how Jim Lerner's program works. The program can read the disk, so it must contain the key. I'm trying to find the key. And one person can do that job as well as fifteen—if that one person happens to be a computer genius, that is."

"Like you?" suggested Joe.

"Well," admitted Phil, "I'm too modest to come right out and say it. . . ."

"Uh-huh," said Frank. "Okay, Phil, we'll leave you on the job. But be careful. The next fire in your lab may be more than your state-of-the-art fire prevention system can handle."

"I'll stay on my toes," Phil said.

Frank and Joe stepped out of the lab. The fire trucks were already gone, and the last police car was slipping out of the driveway.

"I wonder how Con Riley's doing on his stakeout," said Joe.

"I bet he hasn't caught anybody," said Frank. "I bet that whole business with the disks was a diversion to lure me and you and Con to the other side of town. Meanwhile, the Stalker set fire to Phil's garage."

"Then the Stalker must have seen us give the disks to Phil," Joe said.

"And then he raced to our house and left that note on the porch, just before we arrived," added Frank.

"Whoever he is, then, he must have his eyes on us," said Joe. "We'd better be careful what we do next."

"What *are* we going to do next?" said Frank.

"I don't know," said Joe. "Maybe it's time for another talk with Becky North."

"Good idea," agreed Frank. "If nothing else, maybe she can tell us who we ought to be talking to."

"Think we should tell Con Riley that he can call off the stakeout?" asked Joe.

"Nah," said Frank. "Let him sit there for a few more hours. It'll keep him out of trouble."

"And out of our way?" suggested Joe.

"Yep," said Frank, smiling.

* * *

56

The Hardys hastily arranged a meeting with Becky at Mr. Pizza, a favorite hangout for Bayport teenagers. By four-thirty in the afternoon they were seated across from her, munching on a medium pepperoni pizza and sipping sodas.

"Boy, I'm starved," said Joe. "I never did get around to eating lunch. Don't you want another slice, Becky?"

"No, thanks," she said. "I ate earlier. And I'm too worried about Jim to have much of an appetite."

"That's what we wanted to talk to you about," said Frank. "We're still trying to figure out why somebody would want to poison Jim. Is there anyone else who knows Jim well? Someone who might be able to give us a clue about why he was poisoned?"

Becky thought about it for a moment. "There are the people he works with. I don't know that he's close with them, exactly, but he sees them several times a week—or did, before he was poisoned."

"Where does he work?" Joe asked.

"Digital Delights," she said. "It's a computer store in downtown Bayport."

"I've seen it," said Frank. "What does he do there?"

"He's a salesman," Becky said. "They hired him part-time because he knows so much about computers and he's good with people. The customers love him. He's very patient with them. He explains the computers and the software and helps them decide what to buy."

"I guess we should check this place out," said Joe.

Frank looked at his watch. "It's getting late. They might be closing soon."

"Oh, no," said Becky. "They're open until nine P.M. Jim works there in the evening, after school."

"Then let's go," said Frank, heading for the cashier to pay the bill for the pizza. "Thanks for the help, Becky. Sorry to eat and run."

"That's okay," Becky told him. "I know that you don't have much time. Not if you're going to—to help Jim."

Joe patted her on the shoulder. "We're doing our best. Jim'll be okay. You'll see."

Digital Delights was located in a row of small businesses on Bayport's main street. More Bytes for the Buck! read a banner stretched diagonally across the front window. Beneath it a computer with the brand name Workwell stamped on it was showing a brightly colored animated image of a frog jumping in and out of mud puddles.

"This must be the place," said Frank.

"Looks like a barrel of fun," said Joe.

"See?" said Frank. "I told you you'd learn to like computers."

"Uh-huh," muttered Joe.

Inside, computer systems were lined up along both sides of the store, each running a different computer program. Strolling down the main aisle,

Frank and Joe saw video games, animations like the one in the window, screens full of words, and screens full of numbers. Near the rear of the store was a counter with a salesman standing behind it. The salesman looked to be in his early thirties and was wearing a blue shirt with the sleeves rolled up and a tie loosened around his open collar. He had reddish hair and a light spray of freckles across his face.

"Hi," the salesman said with a smile. "Can I help you?"

"Sure," said Joe. "I'd like to buy a PX-3 Model H with half a millimeter of cubic memory and a BVD graphics board with a UXB monitor."

"Huh?" said the salesman. "I'm not sure that—"

"What my brother means," Frank interjected quickly, "is that we're not really here to buy anything. We're here to ask some questions, if you've got a minute."

"Uh, I guess so," said the salesman. "You mean, questions about microcomputers?"

"Not exactly," said Frank. "We wanted to ask you some questions about Jim Lerner."

"Oh," said the salesman. "Yes, we heard about Jim this morning. We're all very sad that he's sick and hope he gets well soon. Are you relatives of his?"

"Just friends," said Joe. "Well, acquaintances, actually. We promised his mother we'd help find out what made him sick."

The salesman's eyes narrowed. "What do you mean, made him sick? You don't think it was something here in the store, do you?"

"We don't know," said Joe.

"Actually," said Frank, "we're more concerned that someone might have done this to Jim deliberately. That he might have been, well, poisoned."

"Poisoned?" said the salesman in astonishment. "You mean, someone might have tried to kill him?"

"That's the idea," said Frank. "Not that we want to scare you or anything."

"It *is* a pretty frightening thought," he said. "But, no, I can't think of any reason someone would have tried to kill Jim. Hold on a second, though, and I'll call the other salesman." He leaned through the door behind him, which seemed to lead to a back room. "Jerry! Come on in here! I've got some guys who want to talk to you!" He turned back to the Hardys. "My name's Larry Simpson, by the way. My partner, Jerry Sharp, will be out in a second."

"Partner?" asked Joe. "You mean you own this store?"

"Yes," said Larry. "The two of us do. But we're also full-time salesmen."

"That's a lot of work for two people," said Frank.

"We enjoy it," said Larry. "But that's why we had to hire Jim to help out. Now that he's sick, we'll probably have to find somebody else."

"Don't count Jim out yet," said Joe. "I bet he'll be back before you know it."

"I hope so," said Larry. As he spoke, another man emerged from the rear of the store. He was about thirty years old, with black hair worn in slightly unruly bangs, and he wore a gray suit with a matching tie. He had a sour look on his face, as though he were having stomach trouble. He nodded to the Hardys without smiling.

"What's up?" he said. "I'm Jerry Sharp. You wanted to talk to me?"

"They need to know some things about Jim Lerner," said Larry. "They think he might have been poisoned."

"Poisoned, huh?" said Jerry, his voice as sour as his expression. "What makes you think that?"

"That's what we were told," said Frank.

"Well, he sure wasn't poisoned here," Jerry said bluntly. "And I don't want anybody suggesting that he was." As suddenly as he had come in, he turned and stormed through the door leading to the rear area.

"Real informative fellow," said Frank.

"Sorry about that," said Larry. "Jerry's like that sometimes. Abrupt, you know. It's his ulcer, I think. Bothers him a lot. Makes him grumpy."

"Next time we'll bring antacids," said Joe.

"Is there anything you can tell us about Jim?" asked Frank. "Does he get along well here at the store?"

"Oh, sure," said Larry. "He loves computers, you know. Understands them, too. He even runs a BBS out of his house."

"Yes, we know," said Frank.

"Both Jerry and I have passwords on his BBS," said Larry. "We log on all the time. And Jim had a password on our BBS."

"Your BBS?" asked Joe.

"Sure," said Larry. "We run a bulletin board system out of the store here, on the computer over there." He pointed at a computer in a rear corner of the store. "Lots of computer stores do. Customers can call it up, find out what our current prices are, leave messages asking about our products, that sort of thing."

"Listen," said Frank, "do you think Joe and I could get a password on your BBS?"

"Just what I always wanted," muttered Joe.

"No problem," said Larry with a smile. "Come on over."

He led Frank and Joe to the computer in the corner. He typed a few words on the keyboard, then invited Frank to type in a password.

"Don't let me see what it is," Larry said. "You should never reveal your password to anybody."

Frank typed something, then moved away from the keyboard.

"Now you're a member," said Larry, hitting a few more keys on the keyboard. "Here's our phone number." He handed Frank a business card with the store's voice and computer phone numbers on it. "Call us anytime."

"I'll call it tonight," said Frank. "Come on, Joe. Let's hit the road. Joe?"

His brother had wandered back toward the center of the store. Now he was standing frozen, staring at the door leading to the rear of the computer showroom. Framed in the doorway, a young man in brown slacks and a sports jacket had turned to see Joe looking at him.

"You okay, Joe?" Frank asked. "What's up?"

"That man," said Joe. "I know him. That's the burglar who stole the floppy disks from Jim Lerner's bedroom!"

7 The Mysterious Stranger

"Hey, you!" Joe shouted. The figure in the doorway looked at him in astonishment, then bolted into the back room. Frank and Joe ran after him as Larry Simpson watched with his mouth agape.

The Hardys plunged into the back room just in time to see the mysterious figure throw open a rear door and disappear outside. Joe reached the door first, followed a second later by Frank. Outside the door was a narrow alley. The mysterious figure was already rounding the nearest corner at full speed.

By the time the Hardys reached the corner, he was nowhere to be seen.

"Lost him!" cried Joe. "What now?"

"We find out who he is," said Frank. "Either Larry or Jerry ought to know."

Back inside the store, Jerry gave the Hardys a nasty look. "Who are you guys, anyway?" he asked before the brothers could begin quizzing him about the mysterious figure. "What do you mean by chasing through my store like that?"

"We're detectives," said Joe.

"We're Frank and Joe Hardy," said Frank. "Maybe you've heard of us."

"Oh, yeah," said Larry, a delighted look on his face. "I've read about you in the papers. You're celebrities!"

"Yeah?" said Jerry irritably. "Well, I've never heard of you. And I'm not sure I want you in my store."

"All we want, Mr. Sharp," said Frank, "is to find out who that guy was. We think he may be involved in Jim Lerner's poisoning."

"Well, I'm not sure it's any of your business," said Jerry, "but if you must know, he's a deliveryman for a computer distributor."

"Oh, yeah," added Larry. "He's the fellow who delivers the computer shipments from the Colossus Computers warehouse, out on the edge of town. He just brought in a fresh delivery."

"Do you know his name?" Joe asked.

"I have no idea," Jerry snapped. "And I don't want you pestering the people that we work with, either!" He turned abruptly and went back into the rear area.

"Do *you* know his name?" Frank asked Larry.

"No," said Larry, "but I can find out. I don't know what's gotten into Jerry today. He's usually grumpy—but not *this* grumpy."

"Maybe he ate something that disagrees with him," said Frank.

"I bet *everything* disagrees with him," added Joe.

Larry shuffled through a stack of invoices that had been placed behind the counter. He was looking for something that might indicate the name of the deliveryman.

"My mistake," Larry said. "I don't think he gave us his name. But you can ask the folks at the Colossus warehouse. I'd give them a call for you, but they're probably closed at this hour."

"That's okay," said Frank. "We'll drive out there tomorrow morning. I'd rather they didn't know we were coming, anyway."

"Here," said Larry, scribbling on a sheet of paper. "I'll give you their address."

"Thanks," said Frank.

The Hardys arrived home to find Aunt Gertrude scowling as she stood watch over their cold dinners. Frank and Joe apologized for getting home so late, popped the food into the microwave oven, and ate their meals on the back patio.

"So what do you think?" Joe asked Frank. "Any idea who's behind Jim's poisoning?"

"Obviously our mysterious figure, the deliveryman for Colossus Computers, is in on it somehow," said Frank.

"Do you think he poisoned Jim?" asked Joe.

"Could be," said Frank. "The question is, is he in it alone?"

"I don't trust that Jerry Sharp guy," said Joe. "He rubs me the wrong way."

"Me, too," said Frank. "Let's keep a watch on him."

"Any other ideas?" asked Joe.

"Not right now," said Frank. "Let's sleep on it. Maybe we'll have some fresh ideas after we talk to the folks at Colossus."

The next morning, after checking with the hospital and finding Jim's condition unchanged, the Hardys arrived at the Colossus Computers warehouse at eight A.M. sharp. The warehouse was a large single-story building on Industrial Way near the edge of Bayport, with a long loading dock dominating one entire wall. The Hardys parked near the dock and walked up a short flight of stairs and into the warehouse. Inside, they saw boxes piled on wooden flats all across a large room. Several metal hand trucks were lying across the aisles, forcing Frank and Joe to watch their step as they searched for the main office.

The office turned out to be a small room filled with paper-cluttered desks. A fat, bald-headed man in a white shirt and suspenders was seated behind one of the desks.

"Excuse me," Frank said. "We'd like to talk to the deliveryman who was at the Digital Delights computer store late yesterday afternoon."

"That'd be Bill Hennings. He's not here yet," said the fat man.

"Do you know when he'll be in?" asked Joe.

"Probably another hour," the man said. "You're early."

"Mind if we wait around?" asked Frank.

"Suit yourself," the fat man told them. "Pull up a seat."

"Uh," said Joe, looking around, "there aren't any seats."

The fat man looked at him in annoyance. "Then sit on a box. Sit on the floor. I don't care. What do you think this is, the Hotel Ritz?"

"Our mistake," said Frank. He and Joe wandered back into the warehouse and found a pair of particularly sturdy computer boxes to sit on.

"This better be worth it," said Joe.

"It will be," said Joe. "This Hennings guy may be the key to the whole case."

"You know what's bothering me?" said Joe.

"What?" asked Frank.

"Why did this guy try to steal the disks from Jim's bedroom," Joe said, "then try to burn them in Phil Cohen's garage? Does he want the disks or not?"

"He probably just wants to be sure that *we* don't have the disks. Maybe he's afraid that we'll read them and wants to destroy them before we can," answered Frank.

"Makes sense," said Joe. "But what could be on the disks that's so important?"

"I don't know," said Frank, "but that must be why Jim was poisoned. He must have seen what was on those disks, and he had to be killed so he wouldn't tell anybody else."

"Right," said Joe. "Jim knew too much and they had to get rid of him. Just like in the movies."

The Hardys discussed the case awhile longer, trying to find clues that they'd overlooked. Finally, the fat man stepped out of his office and said, "If you guys want to see Bill Hennings, he's coming up from the parking lot now. I just saw him through the window."

"Well, this is it," said Frank. "Our chance to confront the mysterious figure. The Stalker himself."

"I'm ready," said Joe as they walked to the warehouse door.

Footsteps echoed around the corner. Joe watched the doorway intently, his heartbeat speeding up as he heard Bill Hennings approach. Now he was going to get a chance to square off against the mysterious figure who had eluded him twice the day before.

But the man who walked through the door was a complete stranger. Joe had never seen him before in his life.

8 Word of Warning

"Who are you?" asked Joe, standing in the deliveryman's path.

The newcomer, a heavyset man in a plaid shirt with rolled-up sleeves, gave him an odd look. "What do you mean, who am I?" he asked. "I'm Bill Hennings. I work here. Who are you?"

"Are you the deliveryman who took a load of computers to Digital Delights late yesterday afternoon?" asked Frank.

"Yeah," said Hennings in a suspicious tone of voice. "What's it to you? It was my first time over there, and I was just doing my job. Something wrong with that?"

"We saw you in the back of Digital Delights,"

said Joe. "Except that it wasn't you. It was somebody else."

"Then it wasn't me you saw, was it?" said Hennings.

"He's got you there," said Frank. "Did you have anyone else with you, Mr. Hennings? An assistant or a companion?"

"No," said Hennings. "I do my job alone. What are you asking all these questions for, anyway?"

"For all the wrong reasons, I suspect," said Frank. "I think maybe there's been a case of mistaken identity here. We're sorry to trouble you, Mr. Hennings."

"No problem," said Hennings a little gruffly. He headed back into the warehouse to begin work.

"Well, we really made fools of ourselves that time," said Joe as they left the warehouse. "So what went wrong? Who was the guy in the back of the computer store?"

"I don't know," said Frank, "but I think maybe we'd better head back to Digital Delights and talk to Larry and Jerry again."

"Good idea," said Joe. "I especially want to talk to that Jerry Sharp guy. He's the one who told us that the guy in the back room was the deliveryman for Colossus Computers, remember?"

The Hardys climbed back into their van and drove back into the center of town. When they got to Digital Delights, Larry Simpson was demonstrating a computer to a young woman and a child.

"Oh, hi!" he said as he saw the Hardys enter. "How's your investigation going? Did you find the deliveryman?"

"Yes and no," said Frank. "Do you have a minute? We'd like to talk to you again."

"Sure," Larry told them. "As soon as I'm finished with these customers."

Frank and Joe settled down at a computer display and made a few halfhearted attempts to involve themselves in a video game.

Ten minutes later Larry walked over to Frank and Joe. "Sorry to keep you waiting," he said. "What's up, guys?"

"We went to the Colossus warehouse to meet your deliveryman," said Joe. "Only he wasn't the guy who was in the back of your store yesterday. So who *was* that guy?"

Larry shrugged. "I wish I could tell you. But I never actually saw the guy you were chasing after, just the two of you running toward our storage area. From where I was standing, I couldn't see into the back. So I assumed you must have been running after the deliveryman, but I couldn't be sure. For all I know, the deliveryman was gone by then."

"What about Jerry?" asked Frank. "Do you think he saw the guy in the back room?"

"Could be," said Larry. "He was back there somewhere at the time. In fact, he was the one who told you that it *was* the deliveryman, wasn't he? Want me to call him?"

"Yeah," said Joe. "Not that I'm eager to have another conversation with Mr. Warmth."

Larry stepped into the back room and asked Jerry to come out. This time Jerry was wearing a white shirt without a jacket, the fabric stained with sweat.

"Oh, no," he groaned. "You guys again. What do you want now?"

"You told us yesterday that the guy in the back room was the deliveryman from Colossus Computers," said Frank. "Only, when we went to Colossus Computers, the deliveryman turned out to be someone completely different."

"So you *are* going around bugging the people we work with," Jerry said. "I thought I told you not to do that."

"We're trying to find out what happened to Jim Lerner, Mr. Sharp," said Frank. "His life may depend on it."

"Give them a break, Jerry," said Larry. "It can't hurt to cooperate with them, could it?"

"I'll decide that for myself," Jerry retorted. "Look, I thought the guy you were chasing was the deliveryman from Colossus Computers. That's who he told me he was. Maybe he was an impostor. Or maybe you young detectives just don't know what you're doing." He fumbled in his back pocket and pulled out his wallet, from which he extracted a business card. "I've still got the card the guy gave me."

He handed the card to the Hardys. It read:

Colossus Computers
Bill Hennings, Distribution Agent

"Why didn't you show us this yesterday?" asked Joe. "You said you didn't even know his name."

Jerry shrugged. "I forgot I had the card. And I wasn't thrilled with the idea of cooperating with you guys."

Frank studied the card carefully. "Are you sure you got this card from the guy we saw?"

"Of course I'm sure!" snapped Jerry. "Now, if you'll excuse me, I've got work to do." He left the showroom in a huff.

Larry smiled apologetically. "Like I said yesterday, I don't know what's gotten into him. He isn't usually quite this unfriendly."

"Do you mind if we ask you a couple more questions?" asked Frank.

"No," said Larry. "Go right ahead. Maybe I can make up for Jerry's bad mood."

"Joe and I think that what happened to Jim Lerner happened because he read something on his bulletin board that he shouldn't have," said Frank. "Do you have any idea what that might have been?"

Larry thought for a moment, then shook his head. "I can't think of anything. Most of the messages on the board are pretty innocent. Mostly notes about computer club meetings and the latest game programs. Nothing that would get a person poisoned."

"Could it have been an electronic mail message

that somebody left on the board?" asked Joe. "Do you think Jim might have read a message that wasn't meant for him and somebody found out?"

Larry looked appalled. "Not Jim!" he exclaimed. "He would never have read somebody else's mail. That's just not the kind of sysop he is. Jim's a nice, honest guy."

"Yeah," said Joe. "That's what his girlfriend told us, too."

"Okay," said Frank. "Thanks for putting up with all these questions. If we have to come back, I hope your partner's in a better mood."

"I hope so, too," said Larry. "And I hope you figure out who poisoned Jim. Something like that shouldn't happen to such a nice guy."

"It shouldn't happen to anyone," said Joe.

Once back at their house, the Hardys called the hospital to check on Jim's condition. He was getting worse, they were told, which meant that it was more important than ever that they locate the antidote.

Frank Hardy sat down in front of his computer and set to work.

"What good will that do?" asked Joe. "Haven't you seen enough computers over the last few days?"

"I'm calling up the BBS at Digital Delights," said Frank. "Jim Lerner was a member of that board. We might find some messages from him in the public message area. Maybe they'll contain some clues."

The modem made a roaring noise, and bright green letters danced across the computer screen:

"Looks a lot like Jim Lerner's BBS," said Joe.

"All BBSs look pretty much alike," Frank replied. "Now I'll just check the public messages. . . ."

"Hey!" said Joe. "It says you have mail."

Frank squinted at the screen. Sure enough, the message "You have mail!!" had appeared.

"How could I have mail?" asked Frank. "Nobody even knows I belong to this board."

"Maybe it's junk mail," suggested Joe. "You know, like, 'You may already be a winner!' Check it out."

Frank selected the electronic mail option from the main menu. The message scrolled across the computer screen.

"It isn't junk mail," said Frank, reading the letter.

"We'd have been better off if it were," said Joe, watching over Frank's shoulder. "Mail like this we don't need."

The letter read:

I KNOW WHO YOU ARE, HARDY. STAY OFF THE JIM LERNER CASE IF YOU KNOW WHAT'S GOOD FOR YOU. AND STAY AWAY FROM DIGITAL DELIGHTS! SIGNED, THE STALKER

9 Stalking the Stalker

The Hardys were back at Digital Delights early the next morning, demanding an explanation for the message they had found on the BBS the day before.

"I wish I knew who left the message," said Larry Simpson, a worried look on his face. "But it really could have been anybody. Our board has several hundred members, many of whom call in on a regular basis."

"But how would they have known that I was a member of the bulletin board?" asked Frank.

"Easy," said Larry. "Anybody can call up a membership list from the main menu. Here. I'll show you."

He walked to the computer that was running the BBS and typed a few commands on the keyboard. A list of names flowed across the screen. He pressed a key to stop the screen from scrolling and pointed at Frank's name.

"See?" Larry asked. "Your name was automatically added to this list when you typed in your password two days ago. The Stalker, whoever he is, could have seen your name on the list and left a message."

"Can you trace the message and find out who sent it?" asked Joe.

"As a matter of fact, I can," said Larry, his face brightening. He typed several more commands on the computer. More bright green lines of characters appeared on the screen.

"Just what I was afraid of," said Larry. "This Stalker guy never left his real name. A lot of BBS users just use handles, fake names, like on CB radio. They think it makes them cool, not letting anybody know who they are. This guy just signed on using the handle the Stalker, the same name he signed on your electronic note."

"When did this guy join the BBS?" asked Frank.

Larry looked at the screen again. "Two days ago. Same day you did. He must have known you'd be on here."

"The guy in the back room?" suggested Joe.

"Could be," said Frank. "He might have seen Larry signing me up on the computer."

"And so he called in later and left the message," said Joe. "It all fits."

"Now all we have to do is find out who that guy was," said Frank. "Maybe we should talk to your partner Jerry again. He may know more about that guy than he's letting on."

"Unfortunately, he's not in now," said Larry.

"Where is he?" asked Frank.

"I wish I knew," said Larry. "He's been getting awfully secretive lately, missing work, taking off on long breaks without telling me why."

Joe leaned against the counter. "What are all these papers?" he asked, fingering a thick sheaf of forms and carbons perched on the edge.

"Just computer invoices," Larry said. "We're shipping a load of computers out of the country for a client of ours."

"Hey," said Joe, showing the top paper to Frank. "Look at this. Isn't the country these things are being shipped to in Eastern Europe?"

"You're right," said Frank. "Is that legal? I thought we weren't allowed to sell computers to countries over there."

"A few years ago we weren't," said Larry. "But our government and theirs get along better now than they used to. It's legal to ship computers there. Times change."

"Who worked out this deal for all these computers?" asked Joe. "It looks like you guys really hit the jackpot."

"That was Jerry's doing," said Larry. "He was negotiating that deal for quite a while. Yeah, we're doing all right. I sure don't regret buying into the computer business."

Joe was still snooping around behind the counter. "Here are some more invoices," he said, "for computer sales to Canada. Don't you guys ever sell any computers in Bayport?"

"One or two," Larry said, laughing. "That's another of Jerry's little deals. He gets around. So do I. We like to think of ourselves as international computer entrepreneurs."

"How did you and Jerry get together, anyway?" asked Frank.

"We met at a computer show about three years ago," said Larry. "Turned out we both had a little money to invest and we were both looking to start our own businesses. It seemed natural to go into partnership."

"Looks like it worked out pretty well," said Joe.

"It did," Larry agreed.

"Are you and Jerry close friends?" asked Frank. "I mean, do you hang around together after hours, that sort of thing?"

"Not really," said Larry. "He has his friends and I have mine. It's a business relationship mostly. I go out to his house occasionally to talk about deals, but that's about it. I don't know what he does in his spare time, and to be honest, I don't really care."

"Well, I'd like to talk to him one more time," said

Frank. "Don't be surprised if you see us here again."

"It wouldn't surprise me a bit," said Larry. "I'm starting to think of you as regular customers. In fact, you're here more regularly than our regular customers."

"Maybe next time," said Frank, "you can interest my brother in getting his own computer."

"Don't bet on it," Joe responded as he headed toward the door.

Frank followed him out to the van, and they drove home. As they neared their house, Joe poked Frank in the arm.

"Ouch," said Frank. "What was that for?"

"Park on the other side of the street," Joe told him. "Something's wrong."

"What's wrong?" asked Frank, pulling the van to the curb opposite the house. "Where?"

"Over there," said Joe, pointing to some shrubbery alongside their house. "Do you see a shadow that doesn't belong there?"

Frank looked over toward the house. The limbs on one of the bushes looked out of place, and a dark shadow about the size of a crouching person fell across the lawn.

"Yeah, I think so," said Frank. "In the bushes. Think somebody's hiding in there?"

"Uh-huh," said Joe. "Waiting for us."

"It must be our friend the Stalker," said Frank.

"I sure hope so," said Joe. "I've been looking forward to seeing him again. Now's our chance."

81

"You go the other way around the house," said Frank, pointing. "I'll block his escape, and you come up from behind him. Be quiet, though. I don't think he's seen us yet."

"Right," said Joe. "Let's go."

Frank slipped carefully out of the driver's side of the van. Out of the corner of his eye he saw Joe slide out the passenger door and drop to the ground. The shadow Joe had seen in the bushes remained still as Frank tiptoed across the lawn and dropped to a crouch near the corner of the house.

There was a rustle of movement from the bushes. A hand reached out from behind the shrubbery and grabbed at the Hardys' living room window.

Frank felt a chill. The Stalker was trying to break into the house, and Aunt Gertrude was in there alone. He and his brother had gotten back from the computer store just in time!

But why? Did the Stalker think that they now had the disks instead of Phil Cohen? Or was he making good on his threat to keep them off the case?

Suddenly Joe came rushing out of the backyard, running straight toward the Stalker. "Come out of there!" he shouted, his voice unusually sharp and harsh. The figure in the shrubbery started with surprise and darted out of the bushes.

He was wearing jeans and a T-shirt, with a light jacket wrapped around his head like a cowl so that his face was hidden in shadows. He darted away from Joe in panic—and stumbled right toward Frank.

Frank dived at the Stalker, tackling him and driving him to the ground. Triumphantly, Frank grabbed the jacket and pulled it off his head, revealing his face.

At last, thought Frank, standing up to get a good look at his captive, the Stalker is unmasked!

10 Guessing Game

"Phil Cohen!" cried Frank Hardy, looking at the figure on the ground.

"Phil?" echoed Joe Hardy, walking up to where Frank stood over his captive. "What are you doing here?"

Phil Cohen sat up and wiped blades of grass off his shirt. "What do you mean, what am I doing here?" he asked. "I'm working on this case, too, remember? And some thanks I get. You guys scared the wits out of me, coming up behind me, yelling like that. I thought for a second you were the guy who wanted to steal the disks, coming to get me."

"What my brother means," Frank said, "is what were you doing hiding in the bushes, with your

84

jacket pulled over your head? We thought you were one of the bad guys, not one of the good guys."

"I was afraid somebody might recognize me," said Phil. "Since somebody tried to blow up my workshop, I've been getting more and more nervous. I finally decided that maybe I didn't want these disks around my place anymore." He pulled the box of disks out of the pocket of his jacket, which now lay crumpled on the lawn. "So I brought them back to you guys."

Joe's eyes opened in amazement. "You mean you're giving up?" he asked. "The great Phil Cohen is admitting defeat? You can't break the code on these disks?"

"Well, yes," said Phil, an embarrassed look on his face. "I mean, given enough time I could crack the code, but your friend Jim Lerner doesn't have the time. So I thought there might be a quicker way."

"Stand up and tell us about it," said Frank, offering his hand to Phil and helping him get back on his feet.

"We're going to have to guess what Jim Lerner's password is," said Phil.

Joe looked disappointed. "We've already tried that," he said. "Over at Jim's house the other day. With his girlfriend."

"But did you *really* try?" asked Phil. "Did you systematically run through all the passwords Jim might have used?"

"Well, no," Frank admitted.

"That sounds pretty dull," said Joe. "That could take all day."

"Jim Lerner's life is at stake—and you're worried about getting bored?" Phil asked, amazed.

"Sorry," said Joe. "You're right. So how do we go about this?"

"We'll use Frank's computer," said Phil, "and have a kind of brainstorming session. You don't mind using your computer, do you, Frank?"

"Not at all," Frank said.

"Maybe we should call Becky," Joe suggested. "She can tell us things about Jim that might help us find his password."

"Good idea," said Frank. "I'll get on the phone to her right away. And then we start brainstorming, until we find the password."

An hour later, Frank, Joe, Phil, and Becky were settled in Frank's room. Joe sprawled on Frank's bed with a soft drink in hand. Phil sat backward on a folding chair with his arms laced across the back. Becky, dressed in a sweatshirt and jeans, perched on the edge of an armchair. She informed the others that she had just been to the hospital that morning and Jim's condition was worse than ever.

The screen of Frank's computer glowed green in front of the group. Frank sat at the keyboard with Jim's BBS program staring at him, waiting for him to type a password. The blinking cursor, ticking away the seconds like a clock, was a constant reminder that they had to figure out how to read the disks before Jim Lerner's life slipped away.

"What do we try first?" Frank asked. "Any suggestions?"

"How about Becky's name?" suggested Joe.

"Good idea," said Phil. "People often use people's names for passwords, particularly the names of friends and relatives. It makes them easy to remember."

"What's your full name, Becky?" Frank asked. "Becky North?"

"Rebecca Ann North," Becky replied. "But I doubt that he would have used my whole name as his password. It's too long, and he would have had to type it every time he logged on to the board."

"I'll try it in pieces," Frank said. He typed *Rebecca* and waited for a response. *Invalid password*, the computer told him with a beep. Then he tried *Ann. Invalid password*, the computer said again. Finally he tried *North.* No good.

"Try *Becky*," suggested Joe. Frank did as ordered. The computer refused to accept it.

"*Becky North?*" suggested Phil.

"That's getting a little long," said Frank, "but I'll try it." He typed the name. The computer beeped its rejection.

"So much for my name," said Becky, a bit disappointed.

"What next?" asked Frank.

"How about the names of sports stars?" said Joe.

"Jim wasn't really into sports," said Becky.

"Movie stars?" suggested Frank.

"We can try," Becky said.

For the next two hours the foursome rattled off suggestion after suggestion, each of which Frank typed into the computer. Becky rattled off the names of Jim's friends and teachers; Phil proposed various words that would be meaningful to a computer programmer; Joe threw out everything from the titles of current TV shows to the names of South American countries.

None of them worked.

"I've got an idea," said Phil wearily. "Do you know if Jim was a member of any other BBSs besides his own?"

"Sure," said Becky. "He was a member of most of the BBSs in town."

"Is it possible," said Phil, "that he might have used the same password on one of those BBSs as he used on his own?"

Becky shrugged her shoulders. "I don't know," she said. "It's possible, I guess."

"Then let's call around to some of the other sysops," said Phil, "and ask them what Jim's password is on *their* boards."

"Now you're talking," said Joe. "That sounds a lot more exciting than what we've been doing for the last two hours."

"Where do we get the phone numbers for the BBSs?" asked Frank.

"Jim keeps a list of other BBSs on his BBS," said Becky. "Most sysops do."

"Can we see this list?" asked Joe. "Or do we need a higher security level?"

"Anybody can read it," said Becky, changing places with Frank at the computer. She restarted the BBS program and typed in her name and password. A minute later she had called up a list of BBSs along with their phone numbers.

"Wow!" said Joe. "Are all of those BBSs in the Bayport area?"

"Yes," said Becky. "You'd be surprised how many there are. I'll print the list on your printer, okay?"

The printer chattered for a minute, then Frank tore off a length of paper with the BBS names and numbers on it. "Let's start calling," he said, using a thumbtack to attach the list to a bulletin board on the wall above the computer.

"Which phone should we use?" asked Joe. "Yours is attached to the computer, isn't it?"

"That's no problem," said Frank. "We can make calls out as long as the modem isn't switched on."

Becky made the phone calls because she was acquainted with several of the sysops, having exchanged electronic mail with them on Jim's BBS. Several sysops were understandably reluctant to give out Jim's password. But word of Jim's condition had spread rapidly through the local community of computer users, and most of the sysops were happy to help out once Becky had explained the situation. Some even gave out the numbers of other BBSs that Jim may have been a member of. Becky scribbled the numbers on scraps of paper, which Frank pinned to the bulletin board.

Finally, after two more hours, all the numbers had been called. Becky had filled two pages of a notebook with passwords that Jim had used on various BBSs.

All the passwords were different. Some were words, others were meaningless strings of letters and numbers, but no two were alike.

"That's a bad sign," said Phil Cohen. "If he didn't use the same password on any two BBSs, then he probably had a separate password on his own BBS."

"True," said Frank, "but I'd better type them anyway."

With Becky's list of passwords at his elbow, Frank typed one password after another. The computer beeped at each one. When he finished the list, he leaned back and sighed.

"This was a great idea, Phil," said Frank. "But it doesn't seem to be working. I don't know about you guys, but I'm fresh out of ideas."

"Maybe there are some more BBSs we can call up," said Phil.

Phil pointed at a scrap of paper on Frank's bulletin board. "Here's a number I don't remember calling," he said.

"What are you talking about?" asked Frank,

staring over Phil's shoulder. Phil was looking at the scrap of paper that Frank had found in Jim Lerner's hand the night he was poisoned. Frank had tacked it to the bulletin board for safekeeping. Frank looked again at the words ShE IS ILL printed on it.

"That's not a number," Frank said to Phil. "You're looking at it wrong."

"No," said Phil. "It *is* a number. Though, now that you mention it, it doesn't look like a phone number."

Frank looked at the scrap. Sure enough, it had been knocked sideways by the afternoon's activity, and Phil was looking at it from the wrong side, viewing it upside down. "It says 'ShE IS . . .'"

Frank paused in midsentence, a chill running down his spine. He reached out and gently removed the thumbtack from the piece of paper, then placed it in the palm of his hand. Phil was right. It was *Frank* who had been looking at it upside down.

While the others stared at him as though he had gone crazy, Frank rotated the sheet of paper and looked at it the other way. When viewed upside down, the dot matrix letters of the words ShE IS ILL were magically transformed into numerals, the sequence of numbers 771 51 345.

"Jim's password," said Frank quietly.

11 A Shot in the Dark

"You mean you had the password all along and didn't tell us?" shouted Joe. "We've been sitting for half the afternoon rattling off passwords and the real one was thumbtacked to your bulletin board?"

Frank winced. "I didn't know," he said defensively. "I was looking at it the wrong way."

Joe shook his head. "I don't believe this!"

"I'd like to remind you guys," said Phil Cohen, "that we don't even know if it is the password yet. And we won't know until Frank sits down and types it into the computer."

"Right," said Frank, seating himself at the keyboard. He started the BBS program again, typed

Jim's name, and then typed the password 771 51 345.

Bingo! The computer accepted the password without a beep. It displayed the words:

WELCOME, LORD AND MASTER!
I AWAIT YOUR COMMAND.

"We're in!" said Frank.

"Great!" shouted Joe. "Now, how do we read the electronic mail?"

"I'll do it," said Becky, taking the seat from Frank. "I know what commands to use."

She typed briskly on the keyboard, calling up the main BBS menu, then hitting a series of keys. A list of names appeared on the screen.

"This is a list of the electronic messages waiting on the disk," she told the others. "The list gives the name of the person receiving the mail and the name of the person sending it."

Joe read off the screen. " 'From Captain Future to Frodo Baggins.' What kind of names are those?"

"Handles," said Phil. "Fake BBS names."

"Like Larry was telling us at the computer store," added Frank.

"So how do we read these messages?" asked Frank.

"Each name in the list has a number in front of it," said Becky. "See? All I have to do is type the number and we can read the message. Which one do you want to see first?"

"Who knows?" said Joe. "I guess we'll have to read them all."

"Okay," said Becky. "I'll start with message number one."

She typed 1 and pressed Enter. Several lines of text scrolled their way up onto the screen:

FROM: Luke Skywalker
TO: Megabyte Max
SUBJECT: Computer Show
Hey, MM, you going to be at the computer show this year? I plan to buy that memory expansion board before I go and maybe pick up a 60 meg hard disk while I'm there. How about you?

"This is real exciting stuff," said Joe, stifling a yawn. "Is it all like this?"

"Probably," said Becky. "Messages like this mean a lot to the people who send them but not much to us. Reading other people's mail isn't nearly as interesting as you'd think it would be."

"Let's read on," said Frank. "There's got to be something important on here—so important that it was worth poisoning Jim for. And we've got to find it."

Becky asked the computer to display the second message, which turned out to be much like the first, as were the third, fourth, and fifth messages. It wasn't until they reached the seventeenth message that things started to get interesting.

"Check this one out," said Frank to Joe and Phil, who had started talking about a series of science fiction movies that had inspired several of the handles they had seen on the BBS. "Think this one looks suspicious?"

The message read:

FROM: ZORRO
TO: LONE RANGER
SUBJECT: LATE-BREAKING NEWS
There's going to be a drop tonight at 11. Meet me at Cabot Hill in the truck.

"A drop?" said Joe. "Yeah, that sounds kind of suspicious. What do you think they're talking about?"

"I don't know," said Frank. "Becky, is there a reply to that message?"

Becky called up the list of messages and skimmed through it. "Here's one: 'From Lone Ranger to Zorro.'"

"That must be it," said Joe. "Let's read it."

Becky typed the number, and the message appeared on the screen. It read:

FROM: LONE RANGER
TO: ZORRO
SUBJECT: LATE-BREAKING NEWS
Right. There'll be another drop on Thursday, same time, same place. Just keep an eye out for

cops, okay? If they get wind of what we're
doing, the whole deal will be blown!

"Jackpot!" cried Frank. "If these guys are afraid
of cops, then they must be up to no good. What are
the dates on those messages, Becky?"

Becky scanned the list. "Both are dated on
Sunday, one in the morning and one in the afternoon."

"So the first drop," said Joe, "must have been
Sunday night. That was the day before Jim was
poisoned."

"And the second will be on Thursday night," said
Frank. "That's tonight."

"Any more messages from those guys, Becky?"
asked Joe.

"I don't see any," she said. "Not under those
handles, anyway."

"Can you find out who the Lone Ranger and
Zorro are?" asked Frank.

"I'll check," she said, typing more commands on
the computer. She scanned several screenfuls of
information, then shook her head. "It's not here,"
she said finally. "Jim didn't require his members to
leave personal information—real name, address,
phone number, that sort of thing—the way that
some sysops do. Of course, he may have known who
they were—but we obviously can't ask him."

"That's okay," said Joe. "That information about
the drop on Cabot Hill tonight gives us plenty to go
on."

"These definitely must be the messages that Jim saw on the board," said Frank. "The ones that got him poisoned."

"Uh-huh," said Joe. "But how did the guys who left the messages know that Jim had seen them?"

"I don't know," said Frank. "But they must have found out somehow."

"What do you think the messages mean?" asked Phil Cohen.

"They could mean that somebody's dropping off stolen merchandise," said Frank.

"Or illegal payments," said Joe.

"Or classified information," said Frank.

"What's important," said Joe, "is that somebody's going to be on Cabot Hill tonight—and we're going to be there to meet them."

"Cabot Hill," said Becky. "That's north of town, isn't it?"

"Yeah," said Joe. "It's in a pretty deserted area. A good place for shady doings in the middle of the night."

"You know," said Frank, "we're going to have to tell Con Riley about this."

Joe sighed. "Yeah, I guess you're right. He'll be really ticked off at us if we don't."

"And we could probably use some police backup on this, too," said Frank.

"That's assuming Con lets us come along at all," Joe said.

"He will," said Frank. "We can be pretty stubborn when we put our minds to it."

"I should have my head examined for bringing you guys up here with me," snapped Con Riley, glaring at the Hardys in the backseat of his unmarked police car. Eleven o'clock was rapidly approaching, and Con was growing visibly agitated, shifting back and forth nervously in the driver's seat. "This is a job for the police, not for a pair of teenage amateurs."

"Come on, Con," said Frank. "It's only fair. We gave you the tip about Cabot Hill, you let us come along for the ride."

"Yeah," said Joe. "We're the ones who cracked the case. We should be in on the end."

"If," murmured Frank, "this *is* the end."

"Okay, okay," said Con. "Now, keep your mouths shut for a few minutes. We don't want to scare off the Lone Ranger and Tonto."

"Zorro," corrected Frank.

"Whatever," said Con.

The police car was parked about ten feet to one side of a narrow, seldom-used road leading north out of Bayport. Through the car's open windows the Hardys and Con could see an open field, in the center of which was a steep hill covered with thick grass and a few trees. Another police car was parked a little farther up the road, partially concealed by shrubbery. Under the cover of darkness, the cars were all but invisible.

Joe glanced at his watch. One minute to eleven. "Almost time," he whispered.

As if on cue, the sound of a helicopter's beating blades floated into the police car's windows. The sound grew louder until the occupants of the car could see the helicopter itself, its green and red running lights glowing brightly against the pitch-black sky.

The helicopter passed over the car in which the Hardys and Con were sitting, heading toward the grass-covered hill. Suddenly, as they watched, something dropped out of the bottom of the helicopter and fell downward, its descent slowed by a small white parachute.

"That must be the drop," said Con. "Let's move!"

Con and the Hardys jumped out of the unmarked car and moved carefully across the field to the edge of the hill. Several yards away a team of police officers from the other car also slipped quietly across the grassy meadow. Con signaled for the Hardys to drop back. Then he proceeded toward the top of the hill, where the object that had fallen from the helicopter now sat quietly, covered by the parachute.

A dark figure appeared from the other side of the hill, apparently not noticing the police advancing toward him. He picked up the object and began carrying it in the opposite direction.

Con and the other police began running at full speed in pursuit. "Halt!" Con shouted. "Police officers!'' The figure seemed to freeze as it realized it was being pursued by police from several directions at once. Frank Hardy squinted at the figure in the darkness, but all he could make out was a black silhouette at the top of the hill, about twenty yards away from the police officers racing toward him.

A glint of metal appeared in the figure's hand. *A gun!* thought Frank in horror. A bright red flash erupted from the muzzle, and a shot rang out, breaking the silence of the night like a clap of thunder.

Suddenly, as Frank watched, Con Riley came to a dead halt—and fell flat against the ground!

12 Unpleasant Surprise

"Con!" shouted Frank and Joe together. They raced up the hill to where the fallen police officer lay motionless.

Suddenly Con rolled over and jumped to his feet.

"Whew!" he said. "I heard that shot whiz right by my ear. I thought I was a goner for a second."

"Thank goodness you're okay," said Frank with obvious relief. "I thought you were a goner, too."

Another officer ran toward them. "We got him!" he announced. "He had a gun, but we got it away from him."

"Good work," said Con. "Don't let him get away."

"We won't," said the other officer. "Don't worry."

The Hardys looked farther up the hill, where a man in black pants and a black sweatshirt lay spread-eagled on his stomach, a policeman crouching over him and holding him down with his knee. Another officer stood beside him, gun at the ready.

"It doesn't look like he'll be going anywhere soon," said Joe.

"Except to jail," added Frank as they walked up the hill.

"You won't get anything out of me!" the man in black snarled as they approached. "I don't have to tell you a thing!"

"Let me get a look at him," Joe said, lunging for the captive.

"Drop by tomorrow," Con said, putting out an arm to restrain him. "I have a feeling that our trigger-happy friend here will be a little more willing to open up after a night in jail. Especially when he realizes that his friend in the helicopter isn't going to be flying by to get him out."

"Anybody you've ever seen before?" asked Con, holding up a mug shot for Frank and Joe to study. It was late the next morning, and Con was talking with the Hardys at the police station. All three were aware that Jim Lerner lay dying in a hospital bed and that what they discovered might make the difference between life and death for the young man.

102

The mug shot that Con was holding depicted a man in his early thirties, with dark blond hair and a mustache. He wore a small earring in one ear and had a surly look on his face.

"No," said Frank.

"Nope," said Joe.

"His name is Blake Rogers," Con told them. "He's a drifter and a small-time crook. Anybody can hire him if they've got a little extra cash. He works cheap. And he's got an arrest record as long and ugly as a rattlesnake."

"Shooting at you last night should give him another arrest to add to the list," Frank said.

"Yeah," agreed Con. "That's the good news."

"What's the bad news?" asked Joe.

"The bad news," said Con, "is that he won't tell us who he's working for. And that's what we need to know to solve this case."

"Why won't he talk?" asked Joe. "Afraid that they'll get him for it?"

Con shook his head. "Apparently he doesn't even know who he was working for. He says that somebody would slip the instructions and his payments under his door in an envelope. Then he'd go off to Cabot Hill and pick up a box dropped by a helicopter, which he'd take to a prearranged address. Or he'd be given a truckload of boxes to drive to a destination, where he'd drop them off for somebody else to pick up. He never saw another human being, no one he can identify, anyway."

"Then this Rogers guy can't be either the Lone Ranger or Zorro," said Frank. "I bet he wouldn't even know how to use a computer to leave a message on a BBS."

"We asked him about this computer business," said Con. "He just gave us a blank look."

"So who are the Lone Ranger and Zorro?" Frank wondered aloud. "And why were they leaving messages on Jim's BBS?"

"One of them's probably the pilot of the helicopter," said Joe. "He'd need to know when to make the drop. But that still doesn't explain why he left messages on Jim's BBS."

"The other's probably the guy who leaves the envelopes under Rogers's door," said Frank. "He'd need that information in order to give it to Rogers."

"That's what we figure," said Con. "But that doesn't get us anywhere."

"What was in the box, anyway?" asked Joe. "The one that was dropped out of the helicopter?"

Con smiled. "You'll like this. It was a microcomputer."

"I'm starting to like computers less and less," muttered Joe.

"You *never* liked computers," Frank reminded him.

"And I like them even less now," replied Joe.

"Can we take a look at this microcomputer?" asked Frank.

"Sure," said Con. "And I think maybe you'd

104

better ask your friend Phil Cohen to come down, too."

Phil Cohen examined the computer carefully as Con Riley and the Hardys watched him. He plugged it in, turned it on, and watched as it ran through what Phil referred to as its "boot-up sequence."

"It looks normal," said Phil. "On the outside, anyway."

"Could it be stolen?" asked Joe. "Could somebody be dealing in hot microcomputers?"

"We checked the serial number on the computer," said Con, "and called around to see if anybody had reported it stolen. So far, no dice."

"Why don't you look *inside* the machine, Phil?" asked Frank. "Maybe you'll find something suspicious in there."

"That's exactly what I'm going to do," said Phil. He turned off the machine, pulled the monitor off the boxlike "system unit" that sat underneath it, and began disassembling its case with a screwdriver.

Inside, the system unit contained several flat green slabs—circuit boards, Phil called them—covered with dozens of little plastic and metal doodads.

"Those are integrated circuits," Phil explained. "Also called microchips. One of these"—he tapped a tiny, coffin-shaped piece of black plastic —"contains the equivalent of more than fifty thou-

105

sand transistors, crammed into an area about the size of a postage stamp."

"Wow," said Joe. "I have to admit, that's almost interesting."

"See anything that doesn't belong?" asked Frank.

"Not exactly," said Phil. "But something doesn't look right."

"Are the chips out of place?" asked Joe.

"That's not the problem," said Phil. "These look like the right kind of chips, but I think somebody may have been making some modifications after the circuit board was built. It looks like somebody's been soldering in here. Some of the chips may have been yanked and replaced with other, similar chips."

"So what?" asked Joe. "The machine still works, doesn't it?"

"Yeah," said Phil. "Don't ask me why they did it. Maybe they were just upgrading the chips to newer models or something. That's fairly common." He examined the circuit board for a few more minutes, then sealed the system unit shut again with the screwdriver.

"We've got some experts coming out later to take a closer look at it," said Con. "Maybe they can figure out why the chips were switched."

"'Workwell Computers,'" said Joe, reading the brand name of the computer from the keyboard. "Sounds familiar. You ever hear of this brand?"

"No," said Phil, "but that's not unusual. It's so easy to put together a microcomputer these days

106

that some small companies even do it in a garage. The parts are so standard, you can buy them off the shelf and plug them together in about an hour. There are thousands of different brands. Lots of computer stores have their own brands that nobody else sells. They make them themselves, right in the back of the store."

"Here's the box it came in," said Con, passing Joe a large cardboard carton. "It was wrapped in plastic when it was dropped out of the chopper, but this is what we found when we cut it open."

Joe propped it on the table in front of him. The name *Workwell* was stenciled in block letters across one side.

"Wait a minute," said Frank. "I know where we've heard of that brand name. It was the brand of computer that Jim Lerner had in his bedroom."

"Yeah," said Joe. "And I think I saw one at Digital Delights."

"Right," said Frank. "It was the one they were running their BBS on. They also featured it in their window."

"Digital Delights?" asked Con. "Is this something else you've forgotten to tell me about?"

"Huh?" said Joe innocently. "Oh, Frank and I were just doing some computer shopping the other day. Browsing around in a local store."

"I thought you didn't like computers," said Con.

Joe grinned sheepishly. "Did I say that?" he asked.

* * *

Frank and Joe left the police station a few minutes later, dropped Phil Cohen at his house, and headed straight for Digital Delights. But when they walked into the store, they found neither Larry Simpson nor Jerry Sharp. Instead, they saw a guy about their own age standing behind the counter, an eager smile on his face.

"Is Mr. Sharp here?" asked Frank. "Or Mr. Simpson."

"Sorry," said the young man. "This is Mr. Sharp's day off. And Mr. Simpson took off for the rest of the day, to take care of some business. My name's Charlie. Can I help you with something?"

"Are you new here?" Joe asked. "We haven't seen you around before."

Charlie's smile beamed brightly. "Just started this morning," he said. "I got a call from the employment agency at nine A.M., telling me to get right over here. Mr. Simpson gave me the job on the spot. I haven't even met Mr. Sharp yet."

"Do you know anything about computers?" asked Frank.

"Not really," he admitted. "Mr. Simpson told me that the last guy they had working here was a real computer hotshot, but he got sick or something. I'm afraid all I know about computers is how to plug them in. They're going to train me, though."

"A lot of these computers are the Workwell brand," commented Frank. "Is that a particularly good computer?"

Charlie smiled brightly. "It's our store brand. We

make them in the back. Mr. Simpson told me that this morning."

"I see," said Frank, unable to conceal his interest.

Joe stepped to the door behind the counter. This time it was closed. He reached out and tested the handle. It was locked, too.

"Do you mind if we look around back here?" asked Joe casually.

"Well, *I* don't mind," said Charlie. "Mr. Simpson and Mr. Sharp might, though. I don't have the key anyway. I'm just supposed to mind the showroom here, until I get my training."

"Don't worry about it," said Frank, leading his brother back to the front of the store. "We're sorry we bothered you. We'll come back when Mr. Sharp and Mr. Simpson are here."

"That'll probably be tomorrow," he said. "Have a nice day!"

Frank stepped out onto the sidewalk in front of the store and paused a few feet from the van. He turned and looked at his brother as the door to Digital Delights swung shut.

"About half the computers in the store have the Workwell brand on them," said Frank once they were outside. "And that guy says they make them here. So what was one doing falling out of that helicopter last night?"

"It can't be a coincidence," said Joe. "There's definitely a connection between Digital Delights and that mysterious helicopter drop last night."

"Remember those invoices for the computers they were shipping overseas?" said Frank.

"Yeah?"

"Now that I think about it," Frank went on, "I'm pretty sure that those invoices said Workwell Computers, too."

"Whoa!" cried Joe. "And Jerry Sharp was selling those computers to an Eastern European country. Come to think of it, those computers going to Canada were Workwell, too. Maybe it's time for another talk with our good friend Jerry."

"Yeah," said Frank. "There's something fishy with all these computer deals he's worked out. And the way he gave us the wrong name for the guy in the back room. It wouldn't break my heart if Mr. Warmth turned out to be behind this whole business. Maybe we should pay him a visit at home."

"First," said Joe, "I'd like to take a little look around this store. Remember the rear entrance we saw the other day? Maybe we can get in that way and take a look at the back room."

"You don't think they would have left it open, do you?" asked Frank.

"I don't know what to think about this place," said Joe. "Every time I go in there I get more and more suspicious."

Farther down the block was the narrow alley down which the brothers had chased the mysterious stalker several days earlier. Parked in front of the back door of the computer store was a large, unmarked black truck.

"Somebody making a delivery?" asked Joe.

"Or a pickup," said Frank. "Let's take a closer look."

The rear door of the truck was open, but the interior was empty. The back door of the computer store was also partly ajar. Frank stepped up to it and peered inside the back of Digital Delights.

"It's dark in there," he whispered. "I don't see anybody around."

"Let's go inside," Joe suggested.

"Better get a flashlight first," said Frank. "It may be too dark in there to see. There's one in the van."

"I'll get it," said Joe. "Be right back." He sprinted away as Frank peered into the dark back room.

Slowly, Frank's eyes began to adjust to the gloom. It wasn't as dark inside as he had thought at first.

Stacked next to the door, on the inside, were several cardboard boxes. There was a name stenciled on the outside of each box, which he could almost make out. Cautiously, he eased the door open and poked his head inside.

There was a rustling sound in the darkness. Was somebody there? Frank wondered. He listened for a moment but heard nothing. Must have been my imagination, he thought. Finally, he turned his attention back to the boxes.

"Workwell Computers" the stencil read. The brand that the helicopter had dropped on Cabot Hill. And the box was identical to the one that had been dropped out of the helicopter! His pulse racing with excitement, Frank thrust his head farther inside to get a better look at the boxes.

Suddenly a heavy object descended on the top of his skull. Bright stars exploded all around him—and he collapsed, unconscious, in the doorway of the computer store.

13 The Man Responsible

From somewhere far away Frank heard his brother calling his name.

"Frank!" Joe was saying. "What happened? Are you all right?"

He wanted to tell his brother that he was not all right, but he couldn't seem to make the right words come out of his mouth.

"Unghrgghlgh," he said when he tried to talk.

"Come on, Frank," said Joe, grabbing him under the shoulders and lifting him off the dirty floor where he lay.

Frank squinted at his brother and shook his head,

which felt as though it were about to fly off his shoulders.

"Ouch!" said Frank. "What . . . what happened?"

"I don't know," said Joe. "I went to the van to get a flashlight, and I came back to find you lying in the doorway. You look awful."

"Computers," said Frank, starting to come back to his senses. "There was . . . there was a stack of computers here. Workwell computers. In boxes."

"Where?" said Joe. "I don't see them."

Frank turned to the spot next to the door where he had seen the boxes piled up. There was nothing there.

"They're gone," he said.

Joe gave him a funny look. "Are you sure they were there at all? You look like you've been knocked around a bit."

"Yeah," said Frank. "Somebody bashed me over the head. And, yes, I'm sure there was a stack of boxes here. They said 'Workwell Computers' on them."

Frank rose unsteadily to his feet. Looking out the back door of the computer store, he saw the black truck sitting in the alley. Something was different about it, but he wasn't sure what.

Suddenly he knew. "The back door of the truck is closed!" he cried. "The computers! They must be in the truck!"

The engine of the truck suddenly roared to life. As the brothers raced back out into the alley, the truck pulled away, rolling around the corner and toward the main street.

"Somebody was in the truck!" said Joe. "He must have been there when I came back from the van— and I didn't even notice him!"

"Run for the van!" cried Frank. "We'll follow him!"

The brothers sprinted around the corner, the black truck rumbling along a few yards ahead of them. It roared out into the main street. They clambered into the van, Joe dropping the keys on the ground twice in his hurry to get the driver's door open. Frank climbed into the passenger seat, his head still woozy from the blow.

Joe gunned the engine to life. The truck was now about two blocks away and gaining ground rapidly. Joe swerved out into the street, narrowly missing the rear bumper of the car parked in front of them, and chased after the rapidly disappearing truck.

The truck, apparently driven by somebody who knew that the van was in pursuit, sped through a red light and around the corner onto a street that led directly out of town. Brakes squealed as two cars in the cross street narrowly missed colliding with the truck. Joe wondered for a second whether he should run the red light, too. But as he sped around the corner the light fortunately changed.

"He's heading west!" said Joe. "Straight out of town."

"Stick with him," said Frank.

The chase lasted for the next several miles, the

115

truck rumbling on its way, rattling down the road at about ten miles over the speed limit.

Finally, as they left the city limits of Bayport and the traffic thinned out, Frank gave Joe a suggestion. "Pull up alongside him. We've got to get a look at the driver's face. There aren't many cars out this way, so it should be safe."

Joe pulled into the left-hand lane. The road was open ahead. He floored the accelerator and began gaining on the truck, pulling up beside its long black body.

The truck driver, seeing what Joe was doing, shifted gears and stepped on his own accelerator. The truck rattled and groaned as it gained speed. Joe tried to gain on it. Inch by inch he pulled up closer and closer to the cab of the truck, but it felt as if they were never actually going to reach it.

Frank leaned out the window of the van and tried to catch a glimpse of the driver in the truck's side mirror. No good. The driver's face was lost in shadows. All Frank could see was the driver's chin and left shoulder.

The truck and the van were racing toward a sharp curve in the road. All at once a car appeared from the other side of the curve, coming in the opposite direction, heading straight toward the van.

"No!" yelled Joe.

The truck was still to the right of the van, so Joe couldn't get back into the right lane. The only direction he could go was to the left—right onto the shoulder of the road.

Which he did.

As the terrified driver of the oncoming car stomped on his brakes and leaned on his horn, Joe swerved off the road and drove down the low embankment that lined the shoulder. Fortunately, there were no trees or buildings at the bottom of the embankment. The Hardy van rolled across an open field as Joe tromped on the brakes, finally bringing it to a stop.

Joe leaned back in his seat and shuddered. "Maybe that wasn't such a bright idea," he said.

"Sorry," said Frank. "Don't blame me. I just got hit on the head, remember?"

"It probably improved your thinking," Joe said. "What do we do now? Go back to Digital Delights?"

"No," said Frank. "No point to it."

"We could talk to that new salesman again," suggested Joe. "Maybe he's the one who bashed you on the head."

"I doubt it," said Frank. "He doesn't look the type. I think he was telling the truth about just being hired this morning—and about not having the key to the back room."

"Maybe he's a good liar," said Joe.

"Nah," said Frank. "Some people seem naturally honest, and that kid was one of them."

"So where do we go now?" asked Joe.

"I think we should talk to Jerry Sharp," said Frank. "The guy at the store said it was his day off. Maybe we can find him at home."

"Do you know where he lives?" asked Joe.

"No," said Frank. "But there's a Bayport phone book in the back of the van. We can look him up."

A few minutes later Frank had found Jerry Sharp's number and address. By a lucky coincidence he lived on the same side of town that they were on, not far from where the Hardy van was now sitting in a field.

"Should we call him first to make sure he's home?" said Joe.

"Not on your life," said Frank. "I think this visit should be absolutely unexpected."

Jerry Sharp's house was on a quiet country road, where expensive homes were separated by huge lawns flanked by groves of trees. Frank and Joe pulled into the driveway and parked the van. A small car, which he assumed belonged to the computer store owner, was parked at the far end of the driveway.

"I guess he's home," said Frank. "Let's ring his bell."

"Wait a minute," said Joe. "Do you see what I see?"

"Huh?" asked Frank. "What are you talking about?"

Joe pointed at the curb on the far side of the driveway, away from the house. "Fresh tire tracks. On the grass. Like somebody drove a heavy vehicle off the road here."

Frank knelt down and took a close look. The

118

tracks ran up onto the curb, across the grass, and disappeared into a thick grove of elms nearby. "Think these were left by a truck?" he asked.

"A large truck," said Joe. "A large, black truck, I bet. And it's probably still in those trees somewhere."

Together, the Hardys walked into the grove of elm trees and looked around. Frank observed a loose net of branches that had been arranged to hide a driveway-wide opening into the heart of the grove. Sure enough, the black truck that they had been chasing earlier was sitting in a clearing, more loose branches and shrubs placed around it so that it wouldn't be visible from the road.

Joe climbed up and looked in the cab. The driver was gone. Frank tested the rear door, but it was locked.

"Looks like we've got Jerry Sharp cold," said Joe. "He must have been the one driving the truck. What do you think he's got in there?"

"The Workwell computers, unless I miss my guess," said Frank. "The question is, what's he going to do with them?"

"Smuggle them out of the country?" said Joe.

"Why would he do that?" said Frank. "Judging from those invoices back at the store, he can ship them out of the country legally. There's no point in engaging in any funny business."

"Like dropping computers out of helicopters?" said Joe.

"Right," agreed Frank. "Or knocking me over the head because I saw him loading the computers on a truck."

"Well," said Joe, "since we can't figure out what he's doing with them, why don't we ask him?"

"My feelings exactly," said Frank. "Let's go."

They made their way out of the trees, back to the house, and rang the bell.

Jerry Sharp answered the door, wearing a bathrobe and his usual sour look. "Oh, no," he groaned when he saw the Hardys. "I thought I told you guys I didn't want to see you anymore."

"This isn't a social call, Mr. Sharp," said Frank. "My brother and I have some very important questions to ask you."

"And I don't have any answers for you," snapped Jerry, "except this: Get lost!"

He tried to slam the door closed, but Frank got his foot against the jamb in time to stop it and Joe muscled the door open with his shoulder.

"I'm warning you!" Jerry shouted. "You come inside here and I'm calling the police!"

"Great idea, Mr. Sharp," said Joe, stepping inside. Frank was right behind him. "And I suppose you'd like to explain to them what that truck is doing on your property? With a stack of Workwell computers inside? Exactly like the ones that were dropped out of a helicopter last night on Cabot Hill?"

Jerry stared at the brothers for a moment, then his eyes crinkled into a look of puzzlement. He looked honestly surprised by the statement. "What in the world are you talking about? What truck? What helicopter? And Workwell is our store brand. We make them ourselves, right in the back room. Your friend Jim Lerner used to help us make them."

"Then why are you dropping them out of helicopters in the middle of the night?" asked Joe.

"And why did you clobber me over the head when I found a stack of them in your back room?" asked Frank.

"I don't know what you're talking about," declared Jerry Sharp.

"I do," said a voice from behind them. Frank, Joe, and Jerry spun around to see Larry Simpson standing in the entrance to Jerry Sharp's living room, a gun in his hand.

"I was the one who hit you over the head when you started to snoop around in the back room, Frank," said Larry, pointing the gun meaningfully at his trio of listeners. "I used the butt of this very same pistol. And I was the one who hid the truck in the trees near Jerry's house. And now I'm going to be the one who makes sure that none of you repeats that information outside of this room—ever!"

14 Superchips

Jerry Sharp's eyes opened in horror. "Larry!" he exclaimed. "What's this all about? What do you think you're doing?"

"Sit down, Jerry," said Larry, waving his partner into the living room with a casual flick of his gun. "Me and you and Frank and Joe here are going to have a little talk. You know, you really should keep your back door locked. You never know who's going to slip inside."

At Larry's urging, Frank and Joe stepped into the living room and looked briefly around. The room was large and furnished in a sleek modern style, with low sofas and chairs covered in dark leather, glass and chrome tables, and walls filled with electronic equipment. An entire wall of stereo and video hardware, decked out in reflective black plastic, looked down at them from the far end of the room. Against an adjoining wall was a long desk covered with computer equipment bearing the Workwell brand name. Hanging on a third wall was an abstract neon sculpture that flashed on and off in red, green, and blue patterns.

Larry Simpson stood next to the sofa and put his foot up on the low armrest without bothering to take off his dirt-spattered shoe. He smiled and pointed his gun at Frank, Joe, and Jerry in turn. Joe closed the door at Larry's request, then stepped to the center of the room, near Frank. Jerry remained near the wall, just under the neon sculpture, a looked of stunned disbelief on his face.

"I don't suppose you'd mind answering a couple of questions," asked Frank, keeping an eye on Simpson's gun.

"Why not?" said Larry. "Seeing as how they'll be the last ones you'll ever ask. I suppose I should consider it a privilege to be grilled by the famous Hardy brothers. I really do admire you fellows. And I'm quite proud to be responsible for the first case that you boys were unable to solve."

"Why are you having computers flown in by helicopter?" asked Joe. "Are you smuggling computers?"

"No," said the smiling Simpson. "Not computers. Chips."

"Microchips?" asked Frank.

"Superchips," said Larry. "A new breed of inte-

123

grated circuit that will revolutionize the microcomputer world—and which has made me a bundle of money."

"What are you talking about?" asked Jerry Sharp, watching the conversation with a look of astonishment. "What superchips? You and I are computer dealers, not computer scientists."

"It's just a little sideline I lucked into," said Larry. "And the scientists responsible don't even work in this country. They're in Montreal, at a small university with top-notch physics and engineering departments."

"Does this have something to do with the computers that you were shipping to Canada?" asked Joe.

"Very smart," said Larry. "I can see that I'll be ending a great detective career."

"The scientists at that university must have come up with something pretty special," said Frank.

Larry nodded. "They'd discovered a new type of superconductor."

"Superconductor?" asked Joe.

"Right," said Frank. "I've read about them. Superconductors are substances that conduct electricity really well. So well that you can use them to build super-high-speed computers, millions of times faster than the ones you sell at Digital Delights. But I thought scientists had discovered superconductors a long time ago, back around the turn of the century, and that there were problems with using them to make computers."

"That's right," said Larry. "The problem was that those superconductors worked only at extremely low temperatures, so low that they had to be immersed in liquid helium. You can't make microcomputers out of them. The superconductors discovered in Montreal work at ordinary room temperature. That's what makes them so special."

"If this discovery is so revolutionary," said Joe, "how come we've never heard about it?"

"I bet the Canadian government clapped a lid on it," suggested Frank. "Made all of the research top secret."

"Yes, bless their hearts," said Larry. "Which opened the field for audacious businessmen like myself."

"You mean slimy smugglers, don't you?" snapped Joe.

"Is it my fault the Canadians don't recognize the commercial potential of their own discovery?" said Larry. "They have this crazy notion that the superconductors should be used by the government and the military first. So they've built a secret laboratory to turn out superconducting microchips—superchips—and run them through rigorous tests. Meanwhile, the whole thing is top secret."

"I think I see what you were up to," said Frank. "Those invoices for computers being sent to Eastern Europe—"

"But—but that was *my* deal," sputtered Jerry. "I arranged for those computers to be exported to

Europe. It was a perfectly legitimate business arrangement."

"Yes, it was," said Larry. "But, like I told you, I made a little deal on the side. I was approached by representatives of the country you were sending the computers to. They sounded me out on a few issues and decided I would probably be a little more receptive to their offer than you would be."

"Offer?" asked Jerry. "What offer?"

"An offer to smuggle superchips," said Joe.

"They had a spy in the Canadian laboratory," said Larry, "who was stealing superchips for them. They needed somebody to get them out of the country."

"So you shipped batches of Workwell computers to the spy," said Frank. "He pulled out all the old chips and soldered in the superchips."

"And you shipped them off to Europe with the new chips inside," said Joe.

"Why not?" said Larry. "We already had a perfectly legitimate shipping arrangement."

"But why not smuggle them right out of Canada? Why bother going through the U.S. at all?"

"I thought you were only going to ask a couple of questions," snapped Larry, then he shrugged. "Customs were too tight in Canada. The Canadian government was wise to the thefts and was watching European exports like hawks."

"But," said Joe, "it was easy enough to fly them out of Canada in a helicopter, wasn't it? Right down to the old U.S. of A.—and then drop them off in Bayport by parachute."

"My other partner, Bob Griffin, flew them over the border in his helicopter," said Larry, "so that they didn't have to go through customs with the superchips installed."

"Who's Bob Griffin?" asked Frank.

"Yeah," said Jerry. "I thought I was your partner. Who's this other guy?"

"You're my partner in business," said Larry. "Bob was my, ah, partner in crime."

"Let me guess," said Joe. "Bob was the Stalker, the guy we saw in the back room of the store."

"Good guess," said Larry. "I might as well tell you, since the information isn't going anywhere, that he was also the one you saw taking the floppy disks from Jim Lerner's room and who set fire to your friend Phil Cohen's garage. When he wasn't flying his helicopter, he was keeping an eye on you guys—and reporting back to me what he saw."

"So who was Blake Rogers?" asked Joe. "Just a fall guy? A two-bit crook you hired to do the dirty work?"

"That about sums it up," said Larry. "I hired Rogers sight unseen for the job of picking up the computers dropped from the helicopter. He picked up the computers and brought them to a prearranged spot in Bayport. I figured if anybody got caught, it would be him. I was right. Fortunately, he didn't even know my name."

"Why were you and Bob Griffin leaving messages on Jim Lerner's BBS?" asked Frank.

"That was an accident," said Larry. "Bob and I used the Digital Delights BBS as a way of coordinating operations. When we couldn't meet in person, we would leave ourselves electronic mail on the board."

"That's a pretty nice arrangement," said Frank. "Even if somebody had tapped your phone lines, all they'd have heard was the screech of a modem. The ultimate in privacy."

"So why did you use Jim Lerner's BBS?" asked Joe. "Why didn't you stay with your own BBS if it was such a perfect arrangement?"

"The computer we were running the BBS on at the store broke down on Saturday night and I wasn't able to get it repaired until Monday," Larry said. "Bob and I were both members of Jim Lerner's BBS, though, so we had arranged to use it instead if anything went wrong. We knew what a straight arrow Jim was, that he would never look at somebody else's electronic mail. We figured we could use his BBS in an emergency without getting caught."

"But he saw the messages by accident, didn't he?" prompted Frank.

"Yeah," said Larry. "He was having trouble with his disk, and he was using a disk editor program on it. He didn't realize he was reading somebody else's mail until it was too late. The messages made him suspicious enough to confront me at the store on Monday."

"He knew that you and Bob were the Lone Ranger and Zorro?" asked Joe.

"Yes," said Larry. "We'd been using those handles on his BBS for a while."

"He must have been pretty mad," said Frank. "Probably chewed you out on the spot. Did you tell him the truth about your smuggling operation?"

"Are you crazy?" said Larry indignantly. "I lied my head off. But I don't think he believed me."

"So you slipped him some poison," said Joe.

"Yeah," said Larry. "I put it in a soft drink right before he left for home. It took about half an hour to take effect."

"Where did you get the poison?" asked Frank.

"From my European friends," said Larry. "Apparently it's popular stuff in the spy community. If I ever had problems with somebody snooping around, they said, I should use it. They told me that it was untraceable, that it was such a new poison that no small-town doctor would ever be able to identify it and prove that a person had been murdered. It would be mistaken for a lingering illness that puts a person into a coma and then kills him. Apparently, they were wrong about that, since you guys knew that Jim was poisoned."

"Bad luck, Larry," said Joe. "There happened to be a doctor in Bayport who used to work for the government and was up on the latest poisons. If it

129

hadn't been for him, you just might have gotten away with it."

"So that's what happened." He sighed. "I've been wanting to ask you all week, but I was afraid I'd throw suspicion on myself if I did."

"Why'd you knock me over the head this afternoon?" asked Frank. "Why didn't you just invite Joe and me into the store and feed us another pack of lies, like you've been doing all along?"

"Too late for that," said Larry. "I know that you and your friends from the police intercepted Blake Rogers last night and grabbed one of the doctored computers. It's only a matter of time before somebody discovers that the regular chips have been replaced with superchips."

"You're right about that," said Joe. "Our friend Phil Cohen noticed that the chips had been switched—and Con Riley is going to get some more experts to look at the computers later today. I bet they find your superchips before the weekend is over."

"So you're going to skip town?" said Frank. "Where can you go? The FBI'll be looking all over for you."

"I knew that something like this might happen eventually," said Larry, "so I've made arrangements to hide out for a while in a small South American country until things cool off. I've got a ticket on a flight out of New York this evening."

"Is that where you were heading in the truck?" asked Frank. "To New York?"

"You ask too many questions, kid," said Larry, waving his gun impatiently. "If you have to know, I'm going to meet Bob Griffin a few miles north of town after I leave you guys. He's going to fly the last of the doctored computers to a safe place, then skip the country himself."

"So you hired some kid to run the store," said Frank, "while you skipped town. You've probably got enough money socked away to live pretty high in South America."

"But you didn't expect us to follow your truck, did you?" said Joe. "So you hid it in Jerry's yard in case we reported you to the cops. It also didn't hurt that you would throw a little suspicion on your partner."

"You were going to leave me holding the bag, weren't you?" growled Jerry Sharp. "When the police showed up at the store, tomorrow or the day after, I'd be the only one there—and all the evidence would indicate that I was involved in the smuggling operation, too."

"That's about the size of it," said Larry. "After all, you were the one who made the deal with the Europeans—and I signed your name to the Canadian deal, too. It sure would look suspicious. And by letting the authorities catch you, I'd be taking a lot of the heat off me and Bob. You'd be the scapegoat, the one who took the punishment for all of us."

"You've been lying to me all along!" snapped Jerry. "Even about little things! You're the one who told me that the guy in the back room the other day was the deliveryman from Colossus Computers!"

"I had to tell you something," said Larry. "I didn't want you to know who Bob was. The Colossus deliveryman was new on the route and had given me his card a half hour earlier—so I had Bob hand it to you, claiming to be this Hennings guy."

"And if Jerry ever met the real Hennings," said Joe, "you'd pass it off as a misunderstanding. Unfortunately, my brother and I walked in on the scene right then and fouled up your plans."

"Of course," said Frank, "it was easy enough for you to throw suspicion on your partner by making it look like *he* was the one who was lying about the deliveryman's identity, not you."

Larry laughed. "I thought that was pretty clever," he said. "It didn't hurt that Jerry has a naturally suspicious disposition—which naturally makes everyone suspicious of him."

"What do you mean, a naturally suspicious disposition?" protested Jerry. "Why, you little—"

"Never mind all that," said Frank. "What I want to know is, do you have an antidote for the poison you used on Jim Lerner? That's what Joe and I have been looking for all along."

"Yes, I have the antidote," said Larry. "Fat lot of good it's going to do you, though."

"I don't suppose we can appeal to your better nature," said Joe.

"Assuming you have one," added Frank.

"Sure I have a better nature," Larry said. "Everybody has one. I've just learned to keep mine in check. And I'm glad you mentioned the poison. I'll have to get going pretty soon, to keep my appointment with Bob, and I need a way to keep the three of you from blabbing what you've learned. Guns are too messy. I really don't like the sight of blood. So I'm going to administer the poison to the three of you now—so that I won't have to worry about you after I'm gone."

15 The Enemy Above

Jerry stared in astonishment as his partner pointed the gun at him. Frank exchanged a desperate glance with his brother.

"Poison?" cried Jerry. "You want to—want to kill me? Why? What have I done to you?"

"You know too much," Larry said. "I would rather have let you stick around and take the rap for the smuggled superchips, but the Hardys got too nosy. From the moment they walked into this house, you all were doomed. If I don't take care of you now, you'll call the police and they'll stop me before I can get out of the country. But if you take the poison, you'll lapse into a coma within a half hour—and you won't be talking to anybody, ever again."

"Why don't you just tie us up?" said Joe. "That would keep us out of the way for a few hours, until you make your getaway. I'm not crazy about the idea of being bound and gagged, but it sure beats taking poison."

"No," said Larry. "Too chancy. You kids have a reputation for getting out of tight spots. It's the poison or nothing."

"What makes you think we'll take it?" asked Frank.

"Because I've got the gun," said Larry, "so I suspect you'll take the poison. That way, at least, you'll have a few more minutes to live. Who knows? You may actually figure a clever way to get your hands on the antidote, though I doubt it."

"Some choice," said Joe. "So where is this fabulous poison, anyway?"

"Right here," said Larry, pulling a small bottle out of his inside coat pocket. "I never leave home without it."

With one hand he removed the cap from the bottle and handed it to Joe. "Take a swig, Joe," he said, waving his gun, "and pass it on. Don't try pouring it out either. I've got more where that came from—and next time I'll pour it down your throat."

"Cheers," said Joe, raising the bottle to his lips. He threw back his head as though he were about to drink—and then waved the bottle directly toward Larry, splashing a stream of poison at his face.

Startled, Larry threw up his hands, but it was too late. A clear liquid flew out of the bottle and onto his lips. Before he could wipe it off, it had dribbled into his mouth.

"No!" he bellowed. "You idiot! You—"

His gun wavered for a moment. Frank took advantage of the opening and lunged at him, grabbing the gun away and tossing it across the room. As soon as the gun was safely out of the way, Joe dived at Larry and tackled him, knocking him to the floor.

"Now, where's the antidote?" asked Joe, pinning Larry's shoulders to the carpet. "I just saw you swallow the poison. We've got all the time in the world to watch it act on you. But if you lapse into a coma before you tell us about the antidote, you'll die just as surely as Jim Lerner will. It's your choice, Larry."

"Why give him the antidote at all?" growled Jerry. "He tried to kill me! He tried to kill all of us!"

"We need the antidote for Jim Lerner," said Joe.

"And we can't just let Larry die," said Frank. "The law has to deal with him. They'll decide what kind of punishment he deserves."

"You stupid twerp!" Larry spat the words in Joe's face. "Why didn't you just take the poison like I asked?"

"Because dying in a lingering coma isn't my idea of a good time," said Joe. "I bet it isn't yours, either."

"All right," said Larry, waving his hands. "I'll give you the antidote. Just promise me you'll let me take some first. Okay?"

"Okay," said Joe. "If you keep your part of the bargain, we'll let you have the antidote. It's only fair."

Cautiously, Joe took his hands off Larry's shoulders and stood up. Larry groped his way back to his feet and brushed off his clothing.

"It's in the truck," he said. "In the glove compartment. Stay here and I'll get it."

"No way," said Frank. "We're coming with you. We've got you outnumbered, so don't try anything cute."

While Jerry stood in the doorway and watched, Frank, Joe, and Larry walked back outside with Frank leading the way and Joe bringing up the rear, both of them watching Larry like hawks. They made their way through the grove of trees next to the driveway. The truck was still sitting where they had last seen it, hidden away among the trees.

Larry stepped up to the right-hand passenger door of the cab. "It's in here," he said. "Okay if I open the door?"

"Just don't make any sudden moves," Joe said, eyeing him nervously.

"I get the feeling you don't trust me," said Larry, opening the door of the truck cab. Inside, he slid into the passenger seat and opened the glove compartment eagerly. A little *too* eagerly.

"Uh-uh," said Frank as Larry started to reach into the glove compartment. "I'll do that. You might have a gun stashed in there or something."

Larry looked disappointed, but he slid back out of the cab and onto the ground. "Have it your way," he said.

Frank entered the cab and reached into the glove compartment. Under some papers he saw the end of a small bottle sticking out.

"Here it is," he said, reaching under the papers.

Suddenly he screamed in pain and leapt out of the cab. Clamped to his fingertips was a small mousetrap, which had been concealed under the papers.

"Gotcha!" announced Larry gleefully.

"Frank!" shouted Joe, rushing instinctively to his brother's aid. While the Hardys were distracted, Larry ran around to the driver's side of the cab, jumped in, and slammed the door behind him.

Too late, Joe realized what was happening. He leapt onto the running board of the cab, but Larry had already started the engine. The truck started backward with an abrupt jerk, throwing Joe to the ground.

Frank had removed the mousetrap from his hand, but he was still groaning in pain. "He could have broken my finger!" he declared through gritted teeth.

"That was probably what he intended," shouted Joe. "Come on! You can grit your teeth later! We've got to catch Larry!"

The truck rolled backward onto the road, then Larry threw it into forward gear and gunned his way down the street. Frank and Joe ran toward the Hardy van and jumped inside.

"Feel like driving?" said Joe.

"As long as I don't use my finger," said Frank, jumping into the driver's seat.

The Hardy van roared to life and took off in pursuit of Larry's truck with a loud squeal of tires. Frank raced the van up behind the truck and glued himself to its tail as it wound its way out of the residential area and back to the main highway.

"How can I stop him?" said Frank. "If I try to hit that truck with this van, it'll hardly make a dent on the truck. The van will probably be totaled, though."

"Maybe we can run him off the road," said Joe.

"Right," said Frank. "Last time it was the van that got run off the road. Besides, he's got the antidote in there, and we don't want to do anything to damage it. Any more suggestions?"

"We can follow him until he runs out of gas," said Joe. "He has to stop sooner or later. Then we jump out of the van and grab him."

"Assuming we have as much gas as he does," Frank said. "And what if he has another gun in there?"

"I hadn't thought of that," said Joe.

"Maybe we should stop and call the police," suggested Frank.

"No," said Joe. "We can't let him out of our sight.

If he gets away, we lose the antidote—and Jim Lerner will die."

The truck had left the residential area and was speeding along a seldom-used highway out of Bayport. Frank sped along after it, leaving thirty feet between the van and the truck.

"Where do you suppose he's going?" asked Frank.

"Probably to meet that Bob Griffin guy," said Joe. "With the helicopter."

"Uh-oh," said Frank. "Just what we need. A helicopter."

"And I think I see it coming now," said Joe, pointing at the window.

Frank looked where Joe was pointing. Over an open field flew the same helicopter that they had seen the night before, heading straight toward the truck. It was about a half mile away and coming fast.

"What do you suppose he'll do?" said Frank.

"He'll recognize our van," said Joe, "since he's been following us around all week. It shouldn't take him long to figure out what's happening."

"Here he comes," said Frank.

The helicopter sped over the truck and buzzed twenty feet over the roof of the van. Joe, leaning his head out of the passenger window, caught a glimpse of the pilot inside.

"That's Griffin, all right," he said. "Our friend the Stalker. I've been waiting for a chance to get my hands on him."

"Well, this doesn't look like the chance," said Frank. "He's up there, and you're down here."

The helicopter spun and headed back toward the van. The chopping of the helicopter blades grew more and more intense. Suddenly there was a violent thumping noise from the roof of the van.

"The helicopter!" shouted Joe. "He's hitting the top of the van! What's he trying to do?"

"Pull us off the road!" yelled Frank, fighting to keep control of the wheel. "And he's doing a pretty good job of it!"

The helicopter soared away again, then turned around and came back toward the van.

"Here he comes again!" said Frank. "I don't know how long I can keep driving this thing."

"You worry about the driving," said Joe, opening his window all the way. "I'll take care of the helicopter."

"What are you talking about?" asked Frank.

Joe began pulling himself out of the window of the van toward the roof. "I'm going up to have a talk with our friend."

"Are you crazy?" yelled Frank.

"Probably," said Joe. "Just keep driving."

The helicopter touched down on the roof of the van again, causing Frank to veer violently from one side of the road to the other. Joe held on for dear life, pulling himself to a sitting position in the window frame.

The landing gear on the helicopter was down, Joe

saw, and the chopper was hitting the roof of the van with a pair of hard rubber tires. Dangling just over Joe's head was a flat metal runner secured to the body of the helicopter. Joe grabbed it and pulled himself upward. Evidently, the pilot saw what he was doing, because the helicopter lifted away from the van again—and went straight up!

Joe felt the car slip away beneath him as he was yanked into the air, the metal runner his only support. He looked down dizzily as the ground dropped away beneath him. The van and the truck looked like toys far below, racing across a living room rug decorated to look like a highway.

"I don't believe I've gotten myself into this," Joe muttered aloud, but the sound of his voice was lost in the roar of the helicopter's blades.

He pulled himself upward on the runner, trying to ignore the pilot's attempts to shake the vehicle back and forth and knock him off. The wind howled past him as though it were trying to knock him off, too. Desperately trying to get inside the helicopter, he reached up and grabbed a running board, lifting himself toward the door.

Once he had pulled himself far enough upward, he grabbed the door handle and yanked the door open.

From inside, the pilot looked at him in astonishment, amazed that anybody would be quick enough —and reckless enough—to climb inside his helicopter while he was flying it. The pilot was a man in his twenties with brown hair and a permanent sneer

142

plastered on his face—Bob Griffin, the mysterious Stalker. As Joe tried to claw his way inside the chopper, Griffin grabbed at the door to close it, but Joe pulled it away from him before he could reach it.

Joe grabbed at Griffin's arm. He not only wanted to scare Griffin, but he also wanted to gain a tactical advantage over him. Joe's plan worked. The pilot pulled back in terror, leaning on the controls as he did so, and the helicopter slowly rolled over in the opposite direction.

Joe took advantage of the sudden shift in position and pulled himself into the helicopter cabin. The pilot lunged at him, trying to push him back out the door, but Joe grabbed the back of his seat with one hand and the pilot's neck with the other.

"Nice to meet you, Griffin," snapped Joe. "I hear you've been spending the last few days following my brother and my friends around."

"I should have done a better job setting that fire," snarled Griffin. "And I should have set one at your house, too."

"Glad you said that," said Joe. "It makes me feel a lot better about what I'm going to do." He pulled his arm back and punched the pilot solidly in the jaw. Griffin fell unconscious against the door of the chopper.

Joe pushed Griffin to one side and sat triumphantly in the pilot's seat. Score one for the boy detective! he thought to himself.

Then he looked out the window. A hundred feet

143

below him the scenery spun in crazy circles as the helicopter floated pilotless through the air. Worse, the helicopter was clearly descending and the ground was coming up rapidly beneath him. Joe's stomach rose up inside his throat.

Looking at the controls, he realized he hadn't the foggiest idea how to land a helicopter—and if he didn't figure out how in a hurry, he was going to crash!

16 Rough Landing

Joe grabbed at the controls in front of him, desperately trying to figure out what they did. He pushed and pulled—and the helicopter started spinning around worse than ever.

"Great!" he muttered to himself. "What am I supposed to do now? Jump?"

Bob Griffin, lying slumped against the door of the helicopter, emitted a loud groan. Joe grabbed him by the collar and shook him violently.

"Wake up!" he shouted in Griffin's face. "You've got to land this thing!"

"Wha—?" Griffin sputtered whoozily. "Wha—talkin'—'bout?"

"We're about to crash!" Joe yelled. "I don't know how to fly a helicopter. Wake up and do something!"

Griffin's eyes fluttered open. Joe pointed his head toward the front window, and Griffin stared through it vacantly. Outside, the ground spun in and out of view as the helicopter rotated, growing closer each time they saw it.

Slowly Griffin came back to awareness, his brow furrowing with concern. "Crash?" he mumbled. "We're going to—we're going to crash?"

"That's right," said Joe, grabbing his hands and placing them forcibly on the controls. "And you're going to get us back down, right?"

"Get us back—down?" said Griffin. Though he was not fully conscious yet, his hands gripped the controls as though they knew what they were doing. With automatic, almost robotlike movements, he began to fly the helicopter.

Straight down.

For one or two seconds the helicopter seemed to plummet toward the ground, leaving Joe's stomach somewhere far above it in the sky. Then Griffin got it back under control and put it down in the middle of a field. Hard.

So hard was the landing that the helicopter promptly tipped over on one side, almost dumping Joe out the door. The blades struck the earth with a loud mangling noise, and Joe held onto his seat as tightly as he could. He found himself thrown against the helicopter door, with Bob Griffin directly underneath him.

Fearing that the fuel tanks might explode, Joe

146

grabbed the semiconscious Griffin and pulled him toward the chopper's other door, which was now directly above them. He pushed the door open and climbed out, pulling Griffin with him. Once outside the helicopter, he carried Griffin twenty feet away and then collapsed to the ground himself.

As though from nowhere, the black truck came speeding by on the highway, no more than twenty yards away. Frank was still in close pursuit in the van. All at once Larry Simpson pulled the truck off the road and braked to a stop in the middle of the field, not far from the wreckage of the helicopter. Frank pulled off the road next to the truck and climbed out of the van.

Simpson leapt out of the cab a few feet away from Frank. There was a rifle in his hand, and he leveled it at Frank.

"All right!" he screamed. "You guys have fouled up things enough. This time I'm going to take care of you for good!"

"What's the point?" shouted Frank. "Your smuggling operation is over, Simpson! Jerry's probably called the cops by now, so you'll never be able to make it out of the country in time. Why don't you just throw down the gun and surrender with a little dignity?"

"Why, you—" growled Simpson, looking around in desperation. He looked suddenly less sure of himself. "That's—that's not true! I can still get away if I hurry!" He gripped the rifle tightly and started running back toward the truck.

Before he could reach the cab, though, the whine of police sirens drew his attention back in the direction from which they had come. Three police cars were racing down the highway toward them, lights flashing. When their drivers saw the truck, the van, and the helicopter, they pulled off the road and police officers jumped out onto the road, revolvers drawn.

Simpson leapt into the truck and managed to get the engine running again, but before he could pull back onto the highway, three police cruisers pulled directly into his path. For a moment it looked as though he were considering pushing the cruisers out of the way with the truck, then he abandoned the idea. One of the officers forced open the door to the truck, and a second led Larry away at gunpoint.

One of the officers at the scene was Con Riley. He walked to where Joe was lying, glanced over at Frank, and said, "Somehow I thought I'd find you boys here. We got a report earlier of a van getting run off the road and I recognized your license number. Then we got this call from some guy named Jerry Sharp, who said you two were chasing a truck up Interstate Seventy-eight. I figured you'd need some help, especially when I got out here and saw that helicopter playing loop-the-loop. How's my case coming?"

148

"Real good, Con," said Joe. "I think we've got it cracked."

Con looked over at the other officers as they handcuffed Larry Simpson and led him to one of the police cars. Bob Griffin, still lying on the ground where Joe had dumped him, emitted a low moan.

"I hope you're planning to tell me everything that happened," said Con to Joe.

"Why, Con," said Joe, giving the officer his best wide-eyed look. "We always tell you everything! You know that!"

The next day Frank and Joe stood in the corridor of Bayport General Hospital as Becky North pushed the wheelchair toward them. Jim Lerner's mother stood behind her, beaming with pride, her eyes shedding tears of happiness. When she saw Frank and Joe, she nodded to them in appreciation for their help.

In the wheelchair Jim Lerner looked up sleepily at the Hardys. He was dressed in a hospital gown, with a plaid blanket draped over his shoulders.

"Hi, Frank," he said drowsily, smiling. "And you must be the mysterious brother, Joe. Good to see you."

"It's good to see *you*, Jim," said Frank. "You don't know how good."

"They tell me I was out of it for nearly five days," said Jim. "I'm afraid I'm still a little out of it now,

149

but the doctor says I'll come around in a couple of days. I should be good as new in a week or two."

"Dr. Madison says the antidote worked like a charm," Becky told them. "Thanks to you guys."

Joe shrugged modestly. "All in a day's work. We found the antidote in the glove compartment of Larry Simpson's truck, just where he said it would be. He'd already taken a couple of swigs out of it himself."

"The last thing I remember," said Jim, "was tearing a copy of my password off a piece of paper where I'd printed it out. I realized that I must have been poisoned, and I figured that Larry Simpson must have done it. My only hope was that somebody would figure out how to use the password and read the messages on the disks—and that the messages would lead them to Simpson."

"Too bad you didn't put a sign on your password saying This End Up," Joe said, laughing. "My genius brother couldn't figure out how to read it."

Frank blushed. "Anyone can make a mistake. How about the time that you—"

"Frank! Joe!" interrupted Becky. "You both did your best to save Jim's life, and we're both grateful to you. Please don't fight about it!"

Phil Cohen, who had been watching the conversation at a distance, stepped up beside Frank and Joe. "Er, excuse me, Jim, but my name's Phil Cohen. I've really been looking forward to meeting you."

"Right," said Jim. "Becky told me that you were a real help in solving the case. I want to thank you."

"No problem," said Phil. "And when you're feeling better, I'd like a chance to talk to you. I've got some questions about the encryption procedures you used on those disks. They were really impressive."

"Wow!" shouted Joe. "I hope you realize what a compliment this is, Jim, to have Phil Cohen asking you questions about computers!"

"Hey," said Phil. "I know when I'm in the presence of a master. By the way, Joe, if you've got some time later, you can stop by my workshop and we can start those computer lessons you asked me to give you."

"Computer lessons?" asked Frank, his curiosity piqued. "Joe asked you to give him computer lessons? My *brother*, Joe?"

Joe's face turned a bright red. "Did you have to mention that in front of Frank?" he snapped. "It's just between the two of us, okay?"

"Your *brother*, Joe," Phil said to Frank, ignoring Joe's embarrassment. "He realized that he was beginning to get a little behind the times as a detective, and he asked me to show him a few things about computers."

Frank gave Joe an amused look. "I thought you didn't want to learn anything while you were on vacation."

"Who said anything about learning?" asked Joe,

still blushing. "When Phil's not looking, I'm going to stick a computer game in his disk drive."

"I think we just finished playing the most exciting computer game I've ever seen," said Frank.

"And I think we all won," said Jim Lerner with a smile.